Hey, Becca, yo
I can't even in
It's a little late
If Harvey and

I wonder why
happiest. I wo
to be with the
wanting it to b
I knew that an
myself…

Sorry this lette
A lot of stuff h
I do have one
I haven't told

But the day af

Dear Becca,

Hello. It's been a really long time since I last wrote.
Umm…ahem. Sorry. It's been so long, I'm getting ner
So, guess where we're heading now?
Get this—it's the Church capital.
I remember you used to tell me about the capital all th
(and you always sounded really proud for some reaso
You said it had lots of black spires, and its cathedral w
of times bigger than the central Easterbury one (I'm n
that…), and one whole wall of the cathedral was mad
stained glass. And that's where I'm going right now. C
One reason is that our good friend Beatrix (She looks
like you, Becca! She's so pretty!) is being held prisoner
And the other reason is that—get this—my… Um…
My…well, somebody who might be related to me
might be there…maybe…
Oh, but, you know, he might not be.
I'm pretty sure I'm being tricked, you know?
But Harvey says he hopes it's true.
He says it'd be nice if I still had blood relatives left.

ır father…um, what was…he like?
agine my own father.
or someone like that to show up now…
the Corporal are with me, I don't need anyone else!

time won't just stand still for me at the point when I was
der if I'm greedier now than I was back when I just wished
n as long as I could. I keep stretching that "as long" out,
e a little longer, a little longer… Even though I thought
end would come someday, and I thought I'd prepared

r ended up only talking about depressing things.
as happened lately, and I'm still pretty confused about it.
nore thing to talk about that's a little more cheerful.
nyone yet…and I kind of doubt anyone's realized, either…

er tomorrow, I'm going to turn seventeen.

KIELI

The Dead Sleep Eternally in the Wilderness (Part 1)

Yen Press

NEW YORK

KIELI: The Dead Sleep Eternally in the Wilderness (Part 1)

YUKAKO KABEI

Translation: Sarah Alys Lindholm

KIELI © Yukako Kabei / ASCII Media Works 2006. All rights reserved. First published in Japan in 2006 by ASCII MEDIA WORKS INC., Tokyo. English translation rights in USA, Canada, and UK arranged with ASCII MEDIA WORKS INC. through Tuttle-Mori Agency, Inc., Tokyo.

English translation © 2013 by Hachette Book Group, Inc.

Yen Press

Hachette Book Group

237 Park Avenue, New York, NY 10017

www.HachetteBookGroup.com

www.YenPress.com

Yen Press is an imprint of Hachette Book Group, Inc. The Yen Press name and logo are trademarks of Hachette Book Group, Inc.

First Yen Press Edition: April 2013

Library of Congress Cataloging-in-Publication Data

Kabei, Yukako.
    [Shishatachi wa kouya ni nemuru. English]
    The dead sleep eternally in the wilderness. Part 1 / Yukako Kabei ; translation, Sarah Alys Lindholm.—First Yen Press edition.
        pages cm.—(Kieli ; volume 8)
    Originally published in Japan by ASCII Media Works, Inc., in 2006, under the title: Shishatachi wa kouya ni nemuru.
    [1. Fantasy.]   I. Lindholm, Sarah Alys, translator.   II. Title.
    PZ7.K1142Dc 2013
    [Fic]—dc23
                                                    2012047818

ISBN: 978-0-7595-2936-6

10 9 8 7 6 5 4 3 2 1

RRD-C

Printed in the United States of America

WHAT LIES AT THE PEAK OF THE WORLD

He didn't really feel like dwelling on the nitty-gritty details of what a hanged corpse was like just at the moment, but he could tell this much: It certainly didn't look like a pretty way to die.

As he took in the *example* swaying there in front of him, he briefly pondered what might happen if he hanged himself. Sure, he probably wouldn't die, but his face was bound to look pretty bad while his respiration and circulation were temporarily cut off, and he might wind up with a broken cervix. Considering he couldn't die from it, there were way too many drawbacks.

Huh ... yeah, I wouldn't want to hang.

"D-don't just stand there like an idiot; help me! Help me, quick!" a voice yelled imperiously, breaking into his thoughts. He didn't even try to stifle the irritated cluck of his tongue.

The man with his neck wedged between the blades of the ceiling fans flailed both legs wildly, kicking up the hem of his long robes as he struggled. Watching this geezer in his black robes adorned with their golden ornaments—his scalp was as light on hair as his waistline was ridiculously heavy on fat— Joachim seriously questioned why the man thought *he* was the one who had the advantage in the current situation ... and yet he was actually being more pompous than usual.

"Hurry up and do something about this! What else do you think I brought *you* back into my service for?!"

The hysterical cries grated at Joachim's ears, making him wince.

"What exactly would you like me to help you with, sir?" Joachim questioned in return, keeping his words polite. Offensively so, in fact. He made a show of tilting his head in confusion.

"What would I...?! Damn you! Have your eyes rotted like the rest of you?!" the old man shrieked even louder, enraged. "Obviously I want you to get me down from—"

"You see, the thing is"—Joachim interrupted him in the same matter-of-fact tone he might use to discuss the weather—"you're already dead."

He jerked his chin at what was behind the old man to illustrate his point. Stunned speechless, the geezer stopped struggling and very nervously turned to look. His head twisted around between the fan blades at an angle that looked quite unnatural on a human body, and a beat later the rest of his body swung limply to follow it, until all of him faced the other direction.

Behind that old man, who looked faintly transparent in the darkness, dangled the corpse of an old man with the same face. His neck was caught between the propellers of the room's two ceiling fans where their orbits met each other; his darkened, bloated face was frozen in a mask of pain, and a mixture of blood and froth and drool dripped from both corners of his half-open mouth (*Aw, I really didn't want to think about the gritty details...*). A dull *screech-screech-screech* echoed faintly in the dimness overhead, as though the ceiling fans were trying to snap apart the obstruction and keep on turning.

Staring at his own corpse, the old man babbled garbled variations of the same words in strings. "Wha...what wha-wha-wha what's..."

Slither...

And that was when a bunch of people-shaped *things* appeared.

The color of darkness, they seemed to bleed out of the room's own darkness from every direction. The old man's face twitched with shock as they gathered at his feet, squirming along the floor on all fours until they reached up with thin, eerily long arms like bony tentacles, twined them around his legs and torso and, one by one, began to climb. The old man's blood-shot eyes widened in terror.

The people-shapes opened their mouths in unison and tore into his spirit body. The body's severed legs and hands dissolved into black static, vanishing into nothingness.

"What...h-help me, please, help me! I don't want to die yet! Help me...!"

"As I said, sir, that's impossible. Didn't I just tell you?" Joachim shot a disgusted look at the old man pawing the air, clearly unwilling to let go. *Why didn't he get that the first time? Has he got as few brain cells inside his head as he has hairs on top of it?*

The Elder's face, contorted with shock and fear and despair—

"You're already dead."

—disappeared into the gaping-wide mouth of a person-shape, swallowed whole. Fragments shattered into static.

Tasty... Tasty...

Their low, thin whispers and the smacking noises they made gobbling up what remained of the ghost sank through the air down to the floor, as if the sounds themselves had weight.

*　　*　　*

Tasty… Chubby, fatty souls are tasty…
Souls that scream "I don't want to die" are tasty…

Then, when they had sucked up all of the geezer's spirit, the people-shapes' attention turned to Joachim. Joachim spared a glance at them as they crawled toward him and gave a little shrug of his shoulders. *Aha,* he thought. *So these guys were behind all those* incidents, *eh? Now I can see why everyone's whispering about assassins on the loose.* The capital people never wanted to acknowledge the existence of things like these.

They were at his feet now. Drawing their faces close, they made sniffing gestures, as if they were smelling him. The heads of the people-shapes twisted like warm taffy until they all took on the faces of the geezer they'd just eaten, lining up their annoying bald heads side by side and beginning to all clamor together.

You're… an Undying.
Your jewel doesn't smell good. It doesn't seem tasty.
We can't eat you. There's no soul to eat.
We can't eat you, so you're boring…

The bald old men slithered away from him, all rasping complaints as they went.

"Gee, sorry for tasting so nasty," Joachim spat, but the voices that could have answered him were already gone. His own lone voice echoed hollowly in the now-ownerless office and died away into nothing.

It may have been a clergyman's office, but it was far from anything you could describe as "simple" or "stoic"; every corner was embellished with expensive-looking yet tasteless furniture, paintings, and the like. He sank into the ridiculously large visitors' sofa (which was so soft, he sank ridiculously far down), leaned his head back, and gazed up at the swaying legs of the corpse above him. *Plip...plip...plip...* Trails of saliva-clouded blood dribbled to the floor to form a spreading puddle there. Two cloudy eyes, widened reproachfully but not quite focusing on the same point, looked down on him from the ceiling.

"Dammit...*I'm* the one who's bored here. Now the work I was going to do is gone." Joachim sighed. "How many senile old geezers are left that haven't kicked the bucket yet?" he grumbled to himself, calling to mind the bald heads of each senile old geezer who was still out there in turn. A few of them might have protested that they weren't bald, but their hair covered maybe ten or twenty percent of their heads at most, so it wasn't like there was a big difference.

At the very end of the list, one guy sprang to mind who wasn't bald. Yet, anyway.

"Father Sigri, eh?"

He murmured a name that went with the face in his head, and then—

"...Ha-ha-ha."

He couldn't really say why, but all of a sudden he was laughing. A fit of coughing accompanied the laugh, and he spat up a soggy hunk of organ meat into the hand covering his mouth. It looked just like a rat run over by a car. It danced around in his palm like a pack of maggots for a while, covered in his viscous blood, and then abruptly shriveled up. "Dammit…" For a moment his vision darkened and he felt dizzy. He leaned against the back of the sofa, took a deep breath, and let it out.

When he looked up at the ceiling, the hanged corpse was still peacefully swinging away.

"Yeah, I wouldn't want to hang," Joachim mumbled with a sigh. His voice sounded strangely flat.

It's not as though he'd die just from hanging himself, after all. If he wanted to cease functioning, tearing his heart out and then either throwing himself into a raging fire or blowing himself up with a grenade would be the surest, quickest route. He knew others of his kind that had died that way after going off their rockers.

With his head still lolling back against the sofa, he put his right hand to his chest just a little left of center, where his heart was. For rehearsal purposes, he channeled his strength into it and pushed hard with all five fingers. They actually dug down to somewhere around the first knuckle on the first go, and blood welled up under his clothes.

"Huh." He nodded to himself, impressed, and tried the same thing again. The fingers of his right hand sank even deeper into his skin. He'd have to successfully pull this act off with this very hand before he went off his own rocker, so he needed to train mechanical memory into his body now.

Okay, then... Practice is taken care of.

So, what shall I do now? From here on out, until I wash my hands of myself.

"Hey, you... when you climbed up to that spot on the totem pole, what did you get? Did you get everything you wanted?" he carelessly asked the dead body above him. The body just dangled from the ceiling, staring emptily in his direction, and didn't say anything.

He raised his right hand, soiled with his own blood and guts, to eye level.

Then he opened his palm wide and squeezed it tight, as if to grasp something invisible.

His hand met no resistance; all it gripped was chilly nothingness.

CHAPTER 1

A MOMENT OF SILENCE AT
THE CHOCOLATE BAR GRAVES

Starting from the beginning of her journey when she was fourteen and counting up until today, how much time had she spent like this, riding on a train? It definitely hadn't all been fun and games, but she'd never once wanted to turn around and go back. For Kieli, at least, so many important conversations had taken place in four-person sets of seats just like this one, even if maybe there hadn't been very many in terms of numbers. Most of the people who'd sat with her here weren't great conversationalists, so the chats hadn't always been lively, and sometimes they'd had fights, too. But all of it, everything, even the sometimes awkward atmosphere—this small box-shaped space had contained everything she loved.

That had always been true, from the very beginning, and it was still true today. There'd never been a single thing here that she didn't want to keep.

... But still.

However. Nonetheless. Be that as it may.

The stiff, uncomfortable atmosphere here today easily broke all their previous records.

Sitting in her usual spot on the aisle side of their set of facing seats with both fists placed stiffly on her lap and her head hanging slightly, Kieli was currently glaring up through her bangs at the seat directly across from her. She could tell even without a mirror that her frown was making creases between her eyebrows.

Why did this person always sit right across from her?

Although that seat had almost always been empty in her journeys thus far, today it held a passenger. He was wearing the same sort of long, jet-black priest's robes as when he'd first appeared before her. Right now, those eyes the same deep slate color as the night sky gleamed bright gray in the sunlight coming through the window. He sat there looking happy as you please, apparently completely unfazed by Kieli's scowl.

I'm a replacement envoy from the capital. Pleased to meet you, he'd greeted them when he came with a replacement watchman. That was yesterday. His thin, too-forgettable smile had blended in so perfectly with his featureless priest's robes that for a second Kieli didn't realize who he was and very nearly accepted him into the group without a fuss.

"Can I help you with anything, miss?" he asked with feigned innocence, calmly letting her openly suspicious glare wash over him. Kieli made her scowl even fiercer and darted an uncomfortable glance at the seat next to the (fake) priest's, the one diagonally across from her.

The copper-haired man there was smoking a cigarette with his tall, wiry body pressed up against the windowsill in a position she thought couldn't possibly be comfortable. The two men with almost identical slim but tall builds looked so impressively claustrophobic sitting next to each other that she could practically see a wall in front of her penning them in. The seats on this miners' train were already more cramped than a normal passenger car's anyway, and on top of that was their biggest problem: These two hated each other so much that they might seriously start trying to kill each other rather than let their shoulders touch even the slightest bit.

Harvey was turned away from the other man's seat, grinding the end of his cigarette between his teeth and apparently doing his best to calmly ignore him, but his left eye had been twitching for a while now. The blood vessel there looked about to burst at any moment. The small radio in front of him on the windowsill was spewing a continuous stream of menacing static.

"Boy, was I ever surprised. Who would've thought that you, Miss Kieli, would be Lord Sigri's honored daughter?"

In his (fake) priest's clothes, Joachim was the only person in the train car who was all smiles, seemingly unruffled by the totally unwelcoming attitudes of everyone else around him.

"Stop calling me that. Stop saying . . . 'miss' and 'daughter.'"

"Hmm? Why?"

"We don't know for sure if it's true yet," Kieli growled in a low voice. Joachim blinked, looking surprised, and then burst out laughing. His guffaws sounded blatantly mocking. Kieli, indignant, glowered even more.

"What, *that's* all? He thinks it is, right? So who cares either way? All you have to do is gladly take on the name. You'll get great status, you know. Hey, that's an idea: Maybe I'll try to marry up. How old are you right now, Kieli?"

". . . Huh?"

By rights, she should have ignored the question. But she'd reacted before she could help it. Now she glanced hesitantly over, not at the questioner, but at the man in the seat diagonally across from her and murmured, "Seventeen . . . as of today."

"Today?"

It was Joachim who replied; Harvey continued to look the other way with his chin propped on his hand and his elbow against the windowsill, pretending he couldn't hear them. Kieli could tell he'd blinked at that, though. She nodded slightly, still watching Harvey's profile.

Spring came to the northern end of the continent much later than it did in South-hairo, but according to the calendar, at least, this was the last day the winter winds would blow—the day Kieli's grandmother had decided on for Kieli's birthday.

"Seventeen, huh? You've really grown up...Okay, seventeen is no problem for me."

"P-problem?"

Joachim beamed as he spoke words she didn't really under-stand, standing up and coming over to the window seat next to Kieli, so by the time she'd stammered out her response, she was being crowded toward the aisle and he was knocking knees with Harvey as he sat down (was the weird creaking sound she heard coming from somewhere around Harvey's temple just her imagination?). Kieli held herself stiff. Joachim propped one elbow against the seat back above her head and started drawing closer to her.

"Hey! Get away from Kieli, you bastard!" called the radio as though its patience had run out.

Ping!

This time she definitely heard something snap. Harvey abruptly stood up from his seat. As Kieli and Joachim both stopped moving to look at him, he stepped over their legs with long strides (Kieli couldn't really see, but she was pretty sure he kicked one of Joachim's legs along the way) and kept walk-ing right out into the aisle without saying a word. From where Kieli sat, her view of the rear of the car was blocked by her seat back, but she could hear a commotion—there were shouts like *Hey, what the hell, cut that out, give it back!*—and then not a moment later Harvey marched right back to them, dragging a

Church Soldier whose arms were wrapped around his waist along behind him.

A naked saber dangled from his left hand.

Both eyes—copper on the left, dark brown on the right—looked strangely glazed, and a dark, ominous light gleamed in their depths.

"Wait, Ephraim—hey, that's dangerous!"

"Eep!"

Kieli and Joachim slid down their seat backs and ducked fast. The blade of the saber plunged into the seat with a shrill whacking sound at exactly the spot Joachim's head had been a split second ago.

"Hey, whoa, calm down!"

"It looks like we'd better give your head some ventilation holes so your moldy brain can get some fresh air."

"*Yeah! Do it, Herbie. Do it!*"

"Stop it—both of you—You're joining in, too, Corporal?!"

Harvey tried to drill the point of the saber right into Joachim's skull; Joachim grabbed the naked blade with his bare hands and pushed it back toward him; and the radio irresponsibly egged them on in their closely matched contest of strength. The Church Soldier Harvey'd dragged over just milled around in confusion. He looked pale. Just as the commotion started to get too far out of hand for Kieli to do anything about it by herself, a low, forceful voice shouted angrily, "Everybody, pipe down!"

All of them instantly stopped moving.

A short but muscular old man in sooty work overalls was standing in the aisle, brandishing a long-handled shovel in one hand. Even Harvey and Joachim shrank back a little,

frozen where they'd been grappling on top of the seat, and looked at him.

"Didn't I tell you little snots I'd kick you off my train if you caused trouble?!"

The shout was aimed at the civilians, priest, and soldiers alike, and none of them could talk back to it. After they'd cringed in silence for a while, the old man snorted and plodded back out into the aisle.

His angular form disappeared into the locomotive in front of their car, carrying his shovel over one shoulder. After the connecting door slammed closed with a bang, the tension in the air finally slackened, and they all took a relieved breath. Maybe some of Harvey's animosity had faded, too; he shoved Joachim away and stood up, then thrust the saber back into the soldier's hands. The soldier sheathed it with a look of mixed fear and relief.

He didn't notice...

Kieli stopped clinging to the seat back in an unnatural position and thumped weakly back down again. She'd thrown her body in front of the slash in the seat to hide it the moment the engineer had appeared. She had no doubt that if he'd seen it, he would have picked them up and tossed them out the window without a second's hesitation.

Joachim, who had shrewdly resumed residence in the seat next to Kieli, shrugged and sighed. "That's one scary old guy. Did we do something to upset him?"

"Don't say 'we,'" Harvey instantly objected. The words *Don't you dare even think about lumping me in the same group as you* were written all over his face. Joachim blithely ignored the harsh rebuke and said, "So, Kieli, what do you want?"

"Huh?"

"I'm asking what you want. It's your birthday, right?"

Taken off guard, Kieli only blinked in confusion. Joachim sat there waiting for her answer with a smile on his face that any onlooker would have taken for good-natured. Frozen, she gaped at him for a little while before snapping back to herself with a start and making herself frown again.

"I-I don't want anything."

"Come on, no need to be shy. Not in *our* relationship." Kieli didn't know what this supposed "relationship" was or when they'd supposedly developed it, but he was already continuing. "Okay, then, I'll give you chocolate for now."

He started pulling chocolates out of the pockets of his priest's robes (though she couldn't think why he would keep something like that on hand), at which point Harvey grabbed his collar and growled, "You. Come with me."

"Eh? What's your problem? Don't butt into the fun conversation me and Miss Kieli are having here." Joachim was still holding a chocolate bar out to Kieli as he was dragged away by the scruff of his neck. The two of them vanished through the rear door of the car, leaving Kieli behind, alone. She looked at the radio by the window, unsure what to do.

"It's just one of those 'we'll settle this man-to-man' things," it said irresponsibly.

They were traveling on the mountain railway that snaked along the base of the northern mountain range, connecting the northwestern mining district to the capital. It was a line that normal travelers hardly ever used, so Kieli and the others were getting a ride on a freight train transporting fossil resources. The train had its locomotive in the front, followed by two passenger cars with seats much plainer than a normal passenger train's, which they'd been told were for transporting workers to and from the mine shafts. All the other cars were freight cars. She didn't think they'd done anything to make the train's elderly engineer angry (or at least, *Kieli* hadn't), but at any rate, he was a scary man who acted extremely hostile toward them.

There weren't any workers on board today, and they had both passenger cars all to themselves. Kieli's group (mostly Harvey, really) had effortlessly taken control of the first one and set up camp there. The observing soldiers were standing by in the second car. There were four observers; they rotated one at a time standing in front of the first car's rear connecting door and paying close attention to Kieli and the others so that, for what it was worth, they never took their eyes off of them.

And then there was one more person. The man who was sharing their set of facing seats as if it was the most natural thing in the world (although she didn't recall anyone ever inviting him) was dressed in priest's robes and claimed to have come as a replacement for their original envoy, who'd already returned to the capital. She didn't know if that was true or false—probably false, really.

I wonder if it's okay to leave those two alone... What if they're having another scuffle? Kieli glanced uneasily at the connecting door Harvey and Joachim had disappeared through. Her eyes met those of their assigned watchman, who was sitting in the set of seats next to the connecting door (he was the young Church Soldier Harvey had stolen the saber from), but he looked away as if she frightened him.

Well, it was only natural they were giving her a wide berth... that was the position she was in right now.

People were saying that somebody called "Father Sigri," Eleventh Elder on the Council, which was the highest organ of Church authority, was Kieli's father. And so the capital had used the (reportedly) captured Beatrix as bait to invite them for a visit. Well, it was less like they were "invited" and more as though they'd almost been hauled in like criminals. In the end, they'd won the promise of freedom on their way to the capital through what you could call a counterthreat, and now they were headed there on their own steam, even if they did have surveillance assigned to them. Kieli thought a lot was probably going on inside Harvey's head, but whatever it might be, on the surface he didn't seem in any particular hurry. So far he'd chosen a relatively laid-back itinerary. Still, there weren't any places they could really go sightseeing in; they just stopped by some desolate mining towns. Not to mention that wherever they went, the Church Soldiers on watch came along with them.

Evidently, once Harvey'd decided not to be bothered about their observers, they truly didn't bother him. He did things at whatever pace he pleased, just as he always had, and he was keeping the soldiers anxious and unnecessarily busy. Once or twice he even played around by deliberately pretending to give them the slip just to make them sweat. While he always had a nonchalant look on his face when he teased them like that, he still somehow gave Kieli the impression that he was having fun.

As if he were carving into his memory each day of this journey that might be their last one.

❦

"Unexploded bomb?"

"Yep. From what I hear, a huge unexploded bomb got unearthed over in Westerbury and taken to the capital's energy tower." Leaning against the guardrail of the deck, Joachim lifted one corner of his mouth to direct a thin smile his way. "Thanks to that, things have gotten a little interesting in the capital these days."

An unexploded bomb unearthed over in Westerbury... Harvey could safely assume it was the same unexploded bomb he'd been told was sleeping beneath that park in South Westerbury. If a strong magnetic field like the one that'd enveloped that park and galvanized spiritual phenomena there had been transported right into the capital, the mechanical city was probably seeing some kind of spiritual effect even stronger than Westerbury had. That had always been a region haunted by lots of ghosts—the city had been built on top of an old burial ground for prisoners from back in the era when this was an exile planet. It was possible that the replica Undyings quarantined in that lab were being affected by the magnetic field, too.

"So, there you go. Consider that intel a freebie from me," Joachim said with a tooth-baring grin. Harvey leaned on the opposite guardrail, directly facing him, and narrowed his eyes at him as he lit a cigarette.

"And? What are you really after?"

"Whatever *are* you talking about? I'm purely interested in growing closer to Miss Kieli."

"Liar. You want to mess around with her because she's mine, that's all."

"My, my, aren't we just casually full of ourselves?"

Harvey couldn't quite make a comeback to that one. He grunted in annoyance and broke eye contact, turning away and puffing on his cigarette.

The air between them was decidedly unfriendly, but the ash-gray smoke swept away by wind and the loud rumbling of the wheels filled it up nicely. The single train track clung to the narrow rock ledge along the slopes of the mountain. From the open deck, they had a direct view of the outdoor scenery— which consisted of a slanting rock face on the mountain side and a sheer precipice on the valley side. If this happened to turn into a brawl, one (or both) of them could easily go tumbling down.

"...Is all this talk about Kieli being that Sigri guy's daughter true?"

"From what information I have, this much is true: Father Sigri did send an envoy to go pick up his estranged daughter. I mean, I used that to get myself here, after all," Joachim said in a strangely bragging way. Harvey didn't know what about that he was proud of. Silence fell for a breath, and the smoke he blew out was carried away behind them on the clamor of the train's wheels. Staring hard at the smirking man across from him, Harvey lowered his tone a little and said, "Joachim, is your plan for Father Sigri what I—"

The ill-fitting connecting door rattled and shook. Then it opened a little and Kieli peeked out with the radio around her neck, so Harvey cut off the conversation there. Shrinking a little under the gaze of the two taller men, Kieli said, "Oh, I was just worried that you might be fighting..."

"Fighting? Nonsense. Surely good friends like us would never fight. Right, Ephraim?"

The not-even-remotely serious words combined with the exaggerated wink he sent Harvey's way sent chills up Harvey's spine. "Who's good friends here?" He kicked at the other man with his foot to herd him toward the door. "Get out of here."

"You're the one who dragged me here in the first place." Joachim shrugged irritably and started to walk back into the car. As he passed Kieli, who'd plastered herself against the side of the doorway to avoid him, he said, "Here. You can have this," and pressed a chocolate bar into her hand (brilliantly casually, too; he didn't even give her time to refuse).

"I told you, I don't want it...!"

"Oh, don't be like that. Just take it."

She tried to shove it back into Joachim's hand, but it was already gone, and her own hand holding the chocolate bar found nothing but air.

"After all, I'm sure that oaf there didn't get you anything."

"Shut up. Get lost."

When Joachim disappeared inside with a parting smirk, leaving him alone with Kieli, who was standing stock-still holding the chocolate bar in her hand like she didn't know what to do with it, the air around them grew strained somehow. *Yeah, I didn't get her anything. Why is he even carrying* candy around anyway? It's not like he eats it himself. He's got to be stocking it as bait.

"Maybe I should, um, throw this...out...?" Kieli mumbled, casting her gaze here and there around the deck as if she was looking for someplace to toss it, so Harvey said, "Might as well eat it. I doubt even he would've poisoned it."

"Huh...? Uh, right."

She nodded and looked down at the candy bar she was gripping, but even so she glanced up at him through her lashes. She seemed to be trying to gauge his mood. Harvey sighed and plopped down onto the floor of the deck, leaning back against a pole of the guardrail for a backrest, and motioned with his eyes toward the spot next to him. "How about you sit over here and eat it?" Kieli came over and sat with her arms hugging her knees.

He puffed on his cigarette, keeping Kieli in his peripheral vision while she tentatively tore the wrapper off her candy bar and took a nibble.

So the unexploded bomb in Westerbury...is gone, then.

As he let the corner of his other eye follow the slowly flowing scenery, what he'd heard just a few minutes ago sprang back to his mind. *Does that mean the magnetic field sucking in the park ghosts died out, too? If the ghosts trapped by its pull, if the kids at that school have been freed...*

One of the things that had nagged at the corner of his mind let go, and a tiny bit more of the weight on his shoulders lifted.

He wondered if he had enough time left to unload all of it.

*   *   *

The candy bar she'd received was about ten centimeters long and wrapped in light-brown oilcloth; when she took a bite, it had just the amount of sweetness that she liked.

It was the day when winter turned into spring. The wind in the northern mountain range was still plenty chilly as it whipped around her coat and hair. Still, since the two of them were sitting close to each other on one side of a deck that wasn't very wide, she didn't feel too cold. The lurching of the train beneath her vibrated comfortably against her rear. The guard on duty was keeping a sharp eye on them through the tiny window in the connecting door (he was probably wondering why they were sitting outside in the cold to have a snack, actually). When Kieli saw him, she winced a little, but Harvey didn't seem bothered.

When she peeked to her right, nibbling the chocolate a little at a time, Harvey was casually smoking with his left elbow pressing slightly against her right arm. His long bangs hid it somewhat, but there was still a faint sore around the dark-brown left eye he'd gotten from Mane that made it look sprinkled with iron rust. In addition to this scar on his face and his missing arm, add his general lack of expression, which could only come off as haughtiness to strangers, along with the blatantly disreputable vibe he exuded, and you got someone who their observers had watched only from a distance so far without actively attempting to converse. Well, other than Joachim, anyway.

While Kieli was still peering at Harvey's profile, he suddenly turned his head to look at her; so she ended up reflexively leaning back a few centimeters out of nervousness.

"Is that thing good?"

"Huh? Uh, yeah," she answered without thinking, caught off guard. Harvey turned away again in a huff, looking disgruntled. *I-is it bad if it's good?* "Um…it's not that good," she amended, and Harvey grunted "Okay" without yet looking back at her. *O-okay?*

Could that mean…?

Does that mean—does that mean he's jealous? I don't know, though.

"Your birthday."

Kieli was nibbling on her chocolate, gaze lowered because she felt a little flustered, when he blurted those short, curt words.

"Tell me beforehand."

"Oh—I forgot to mention it at first, and then I just sort of… Sorry."

"Eh, you don't have to apologize about it." Harvey scowled at a random point in the sky and grumbled what sounded like *I probably wouldn't have thought of anything even if you'd told me anyway.* Why was Kieli the one getting complaints about her own birthday?

Come to think of it, this was her third birthday since meeting Harvey and the Corporal, but she couldn't really remember any of them giving her a proper celebration. When she had her fifteenth birthday in the apartment in South-hairo, Harvey forgot about it and stayed out the whole day (though they'd all eaten cake together early the next morning), and on her sixteenth birthday, he…Right, he wasn't there.

Her seventeenth birthday, this year, was the third.

Her eighteenth birthday, next year, would be the fourth…

The fourth—

Would there be a fourth?

"Is there something you want?"

More short words zinged her way, blurted in a rush, and Kieli looked up from her chocolate. Even though it was cold outside, since she'd been gripping it in both hands while she thought, it had started to melt a little between her fingers. "Mm, not…" *Not really*, she almost answered, the way she usually did, but then she changed her mind. "Well, your p-promise…"

She'd meant for it to come out casually, but somehow she lost control of her voice.

Harvey turned around again and blinked at her with mismatched eyes. He had a "What are you talking about?" expression that made Kieli's teeth grind with frustration. She adjusted her legs on the deck so that she was sitting up straight and formal and glared up at him through her eyelashes as she said (although it came out in a mumble), "Your promise—you st-stood me up at the sandbox."

Harvey looked as if he still couldn't remember, but then a moment later it seemed to click, and his still-swollen right cheek gave a weird twitch. He drew back a little.

"Gah, you just won't quit!"

W-won't quit?! Okay, now she was miffed, and she wasn't about to back down after *that*. He had no idea how she felt, mustering up about ten years' worth of courage to ask him. She leaned forward, crowding in on him the same distance he'd pulled back. "H-how could I forget that?! You promised me, Harvey, and then you weaseled out of it!"

"I don't remember actually promising you—" Harvey began

churlishly, scooting away from her even farther until he bumped the back of his head against the railing of the deck. He was darting his eyes left and right like a suspicious character, but there was nowhere left for him to run.

In the end, he let his head droop, apparently resigning himself. "...Okay, okay."

He turned to face her, scowling and still just slightly avoiding eye contact.

When they were directly facing each other again, this time it was Kieli's turn to get flustered, but sitting there rigidly in her formal position, she lowered her gaze a little and held her ground, waiting with her heart pounding.

The fingers holding Harvey's cigarette brushed her jaw lightly, their faces drew close, and her heart made an audible sound as it leapt in her chest.

"What's this 'promise'?" a voice broke in out of the blue from literally right in between them (well, it actually *wasn't* out of the blue, considering he'd been hanging around Kieli's neck the whole time), sending them both simultaneously leaping backward on instinct and causing Harvey to bump his head on the railing again. "Crap, I forgot about you!" he said rudely, rubbing the back of his head. Though truth be told, for a moment there Kieli'd forgotten all about the Corporal, too. *But he was so quiet the whole time! Sorry, Corporal...*

From the speaker of the radio hanging from Kieli's neck, the disembodied head of a soldier was suddenly sticking out, made of dark-green noise particles and wearing an expression worthy of the guardian of Hell itself. If someone who didn't know them saw it, they were guaranteed to scream and pass out.

"...*What's this 'promise'?*" the Corporal repeated in a staticky voice that was so low it seemed to crawl along the ground.

"It's nothing!" Harvey answered in a nervous almost-screech.

The noise-filled ghost only intensified his glare, though, and asked a third time, "*What's this 'promise'?*"

"You're doing this to me on purpose, aren't you?!" Harvey wailed, reaching for the power button, and with one last "Ah—" from Kieli and the radio both, the ghost's face went jagged and then fizzled out, like turning off a video feed.

"Uh-oh. He's gonna yell at you later..."

Sighing at the thought of what would happen when they turned him back on, Kieli let her shoulders slump in disappointment. So they'd gotten interrupted in the end. The sort of broken, uncomfortable air between them didn't blow away on the wind, either; it just stagnated between them. She gazed down at her own knees, trembling slightly in time to the vibrations of the train, and then thought, *Oh, but, maybe...*

If Harvey went to the trouble of turning off the radio, does that mean...?

But when she shot him what all the books called "a hopeful gaze" out of the corner of her eye, he conspicuously avoided it and said, "Oh, I forgot, I hate chocolate."

Talk about a dirty way of chickening out. "What?!" cried Kieli, whose entire mouth tasted like chocolate. She felt as if someone had whacked her upside the head with a brick. He was the one who'd told her "Might as well eat it," and now he was using that as an excuse to dodge her with! *That's playing dirty! I-is that how much he hates the idea?*

In the end he'd weaseled out of it again...She was seventeen now, and she personally thought she'd grown up a lot getting from fourteen to seventeen—but was seventeen still just a kid in Harvey's mind?

In which case, would this be okay next year? But—she didn't even know if there would *be* a next year.

"...Nothing."

A few tears she couldn't hold in escaped along with the whisper, sliding in a wet trail down one cheek and into the corner of her mouth. A salty taste slid into her chocolate-flavored mouth and everything became slightly bittersweet.

"Kieli? Hey..."

Harvey leaned in to peer at her, looking startled. Kieli scrubbed the tears away roughly with the back of the hand holding the chocolate bar and turned her face away. She told herself she couldn't cry over a little thing like this and make Harvey worry, but a hiccup-like sob caught in her throat all the same. *I take it back. Seventeen isn't an adult at all.*

"...There's nothing I want. I don't want anything. I don't care about that promise. I don't need anything..."

Please, please, if there's anyone on this planet with the power to perform miracles, let us all be able to be together next year, and the year after that, and all the years after that one, too.

...I know. I'm not stupid. I know I said I didn't want any-thing, and now I'm wishing for the most unrealistic, hardest thing I ever could. I must be way more of a selfish crybaby now than I was back when I really didn't have anything.

"Kieli," said a quiet voice overhead. A low, scratchy voice that blended comfortably in with the sounds of the train. "Hey, after we've taken care of our business in the capital...

you know that house by the Easterbury transfer station, where Tadai lived? It's pretty run-down right now, but I think I want to fix it up and live there."

Kieli'd been keeping her eyes on the ground, but Harvey's proposal was so totally unexpected that she lifted her head a little before she'd thought about it. She wiped her tearstained face and looked up at Harvey's profile. He kept his face turned toward the scenery flowing by them, just darting a glance at her out of the corner of his eye and tilting his head slightly.

"What do you think?"

Kieli's eyes widened at the question. "I...I think it's a good idea. Really good."

"I know, right? And at the transfer station the Corporal's grave would be nearby, too," Harvey said, facing the radio on Kieli's lap and smiling just the littlest bit softly.

Southbound along the abandoned tracks from that transfer station was a cluster of graves where the Corporal and lots of other fallen soldiers slept. Harvey'd promised to take the Corporal's radio there when it broke for good someday...but if they lived at the transfer station, they could still visit his grave sometimes. They could probably even bring a packed lunch and a new radio with them, and Kieli could play the rock music the Corporal liked for him while she had a picnic lunch and reported all the latest goings-on. Of course, it would make her happiest of all if the radio never broke down at all.

But...

Even though she wished for it with all her heart, she couldn't imagine that such a peaceful, happy future was really possible. She doubted Harvey believed it either, so why was he saying these things to her now? He'd never once talked about plans for the future before. It struck her that he was talking about an ideal life like that now only because he didn't believe it would really happen, and she felt uneasy instead of relieved. She felt as though Harvey's presence was growing faraway and faint, somehow.

"Okay, then, let's take care of all our business first. You and I both have things to do. Right?"

Unable to just say yes to that smiling "Right?" Kieli dropped her gaze evasively. She stared meaninglessly down at her half-eaten bar of chocolate. What she had to do...she had to meet this person who might be her father and find out the truth, and she had to save Beatrix. It was true that she didn't have time to be worrying about what'd happen after that right now.

"Kieli," Harvey insisted, reaching out his hand at the same time and pressing at her head as if to say *Come on, agree already!* Left with no choice, she nodded, and as she did, the scent of tobacco smoke that should be right next to her seemed somehow far away (though of course it wasn't), and she got the feeling if she turned to look, there might not be anyone there at all, so she couldn't raise her head.

Choo...

The sound of the whistle hung heavily in the air above the tracks behind them long after it stopped. *These tracks might fall straight down into a pit before they reach that peaceful future...* Kieli forcibly bent her thoughts away from the negative direction they seemed determined to go in.

It's okay. This smoky smell and the touch of this hand aren't all in my head. Harvey is right here next to me.

A little while later, after a (not exactly) peaceful lull where they didn't talk about anything in particular, the train suddenly began to slow down. Kieli, back in the passenger car, pressed her face against the window and squinted at the track ahead. Soon a weather-beaten platform built by cutting away part of the rock slope came into view. They slid up alongside it and stopped with a sudden jerk, inertia yanking them forward.

It was a bare-bones station with only the absolute minimum it required to be functional, as though it had been built to be temporary. All it had was a ramshackle station house and a platform surrounded by a simple picket fence; there wasn't even anything resembling a ticket gate. There wasn't anything near the station, either. She could see only a narrow path with rock faces on both sides stretching up the mountain from one side of the station house. Still, considering that they'd stopped at this station, she would have thought there'd be people waiting here to get on (since the only passengers on board were her group and the soldiers keeping watch, obviously nobody was going to get off), but there wasn't a soul in sight on the deserted platform.

Then she did a double take.

Kieli'd been gazing quizzically outside from the empty seat next to her own; now she put both hands against the windowpane and opened her eyes wide.

There were all kinds of people streaming out of the train and onto the platform from the movable steps on either side of the passenger cars. Of course there hadn't been any other passengers on this train aside from Kieli's own group, she was sure, and a big group like that could never possibly have fit into two train cars in the first place. That was how many people there were. Most of them wore dusty work clothes. Here and there she could see some shouldering tools like pickaxes and shovels, too.

A line of people hazy enough to blend right into the scenery, and long, so long it seemed to stretch into infinity as they proceeded down the platform and up the mountain path, where one by one they slowly disappeared. The only one staring wide-eyed out the window at them was Kieli. Harvey and Joachim didn't seem to pay any particular attention to them, and it looked as if the Church Soldier on watch duty didn't see anything there at all.

A line of dead people…?

Around the same time that the line of people crossing the platform started to blink out of sight like a mirage, Kieli spotted the old engineer stepping down out of the locomotive. He was a short man, but his shoulders were broad; he carried a pickax on one of them, and his opposite arm held a bunch of what looked like long sticks. What was he doing…? Even the Church Soldier who hadn't been able to see the procession of ghosts was watching the engineer's movements quizzically. The elderly engineer left his bewildered passengers behind (though she felt that he didn't particularly treat them like passengers anyway), trudging toward the edge of the platform with his usual grumpy air.

"I'm sorry about this, but could I ask you to wait here just a little bit? Until Gramps gets it out of his system," a man in overalls that matched the engineer's said, poking his face out of the connecting door at the front of their car and ducking his head apologetically. He was a lot younger than the old engineer; she'd heard he was an apprentice.

When she turned her gaze back to the scene outside, the old man had started hammering with his pickax along the picket fence surrounding the platform.

No, that wasn't a picket fence—what Kieli had first taken for a fence was a group of countless sticks. Long ones, short ones... they were all different thicknesses and tilting in various different directions, too, but they were stuck in the ground around the outer edge of the platform at just about regular intervals like a row of giant-sized chocolate bars that all sorts of different people had started eating and then left behind a few at a time.

Those are... grave markers. Lots and lots of grave markers.

The elderly engineer jammed one of the sticks he'd brought into the hole he'd dug with his pickax and started erecting a new marker. With his back to the train, all alone, silently like a man possessed by something.

"Looks like there's a processing station up there..."

Soon enough the tail end of the procession of the ghosts vanished up the path, and Kieli picked up the radio and went out onto the platform. Wind groaned down along the rock slope with an echoing howl as though it was blowing out of a deep cavern. It was a low, sorrowful sound she could easily imagine was the wailing of the dead.

The old man with his back to them was just starting to erect his second grave marker. Kieli cringed a little at that stubborn back. It seemed to wordlessly say *Don't anybody help me.*

"He seems to feel better after he's done about six or seven of them. I'm really sorry; I know you're in a hurry."

When Kieli turned around to see who was talking to her, she saw the young man who was apprentice engineer standing there. He wore the same sooty overalls as the old man, but physically he was the opposite: tall and slim. He was giving her a wry, resigned smile as if to say *I just don't know what to do with the old man.* Kieli had heard that the two of them, the elderly engineer and this young apprentice engineer, were the freight train's entire crew. Their attitudes were opposite, too: in stark contrast to the overly hostile old man, the apprentice was strangely humble.

"Is this place...a mine shaft?"

"Well, I think it would be more accurate to say it used to be a mine shaft. It was a new one they started breaking ground on two or three years ago...It's getting so you can't extract much from the old ones anymore, you see. But there was a cave-in, and it was shut down."

"A cave-in...?"

Harvey had drawn close to them by then, his eyes casually roaming around their surroundings. Kieli could sense him moving abruptly away the moment he heard those words. Shooting a sidelong glance at him, Kieli got the rest of the story from the apprentice engineer.

Evidently the old man's son had been on the development team here as its superintendent, but he'd passed away when the shaft caved in. The mine shaft had begun development with the Church's funds, but what with the out-of-the-way location and all, they hadn't carried out a very decent rescue operation, and that rescue operation petered out with a large number of people still unaccounted for. Now, as they could see, the site was abandoned. Every time the train came through this station, the old man stopped for a while to put up a few more grave markers in honor of the people who hadn't been rescued.

"I see…"

"That's why he hates people connected with the Church, you know. Please try not to think too badly of him…I mean, I know that's probably impossible, but try not to bother too much about it. He's just always in a bad mood. Honestly, the elderly are so stubborn…" The youth scratched his head with a sigh and went back to the locomotive, mumbling to himself about taking this chance to eat his lunch.

As she watched him leave, Kieli complained a little glumly, "Apparently we're 'connected with the Church.'"

"*You know that's what we must look like to strangers. We're heading for the capital escorted by Church Soldier bodyguards.*"

"I'm not connected…not with *them*…I'm…"…*Not connected.* Her denial fizzled out weakly.

She looked at Harvey, who was walking along the edge of the platform. At first glance it seemed as though he was strolling around with his hand stuck in his pocket as if he was just out for a walk, but at the same time she thought he looked lost in thought.

He must have realized earlier than Kieli had.

It was the story they'd heard from the brothers hiding out in the Westerbury slums: a few years ago, there'd been a cave-in at a new mine shaft being developed in the mountain range near the capital, and many of the workers had died. Because there were so many casualties, all the bodies were buried in one mass grave in the capital instead of being individually delivered back to their families.

It had always bothered Harvey that he hadn't been able to save the kindhearted man who'd told them that story.

Yes—this pretty much had to be the site where Christoph had died the *first* time.

Then Kieli saw Harvey, who'd been wandering around aimlessly, and the old engineer, who'd been walking with a bundle of sticks in his hand, cross paths. Neither of them had been looking where they were going, so their arms bumped each other, and the old man's sticks scattered to the ground. When Harvey knelt down to pick them up, the engineer yanked them away.

"Don't touch those! Leave me alone!"

At the sudden angry shout, Kieli cringed with a lump in her throat. He swung one of the reclaimed sticks violently at Harvey and landed a direct blow more or less where the right sleeve of Harvey's shirt hung. It connected with a dull *thump*. Kieli squeaked and automatically started running toward them, but the old engineer pulled the stick back right away, so she stopped after a few steps.

Maybe something had felt off when the old man's blow connected; either way, he seemed to be realizing for the first time that Harvey's right arm was gone. He knit his brow uncomfortably, but then he only snorted haughtily and brushed Harvey, who was standing stock-still, aside to collect his sticks and plod back to his work.

"That's so mean...!"

"*What's with that attitude?! He didn't even apologize!*"

Harvey only held his hand against his right side and watched the man go, but Kieli and the radio were indignant. Someone was trying to help him, and he'd just up and hit them! No matter how much he might hate people connected with the Church, that didn't mean he had to be so unconditionally violent to them.

She was even considering going over to complain to the old man when a cold voice behind her said, "Eh, just leave him be. There's a type of person in this world that needs to have an 'enemy.'" *How long has he been standing behind me?* Kieli automatically jumped aside a step to get some distance between them before she turned to look up at the tall (fake) priest in the long black robes.

"There are people who need an enemy...?"

"Yup."

Shrugging lightly at her obvious avoidance, Joachim continued. "They're the type of people who can't live without someone to direct their hostility at. Guys like *him* who are all resigned-philosopher about everything seriously piss those people off."

He directed a derisive look Harvey's way and pretended to spit. Harvey didn't look especially angry or hurt about the way the old man had treated him. He walked back over to the train without changing his pace.

Though Kieli thought it wasn't the same as a "resigned-philosopher" attitude, she did have to admit that Harvey didn't really have much hostility toward other people...or more like, he was basically indifferent to the pointless hostility other people had toward him.

People who need an enemy…

She looked over at the engineer's stubborn old back as he went on erecting his grave markers all alone. He'd lost someone special to him, and he couldn't go on living without someone to direct his anger at…Kieli tried thinking about what would happen if she lost someone special. *If the Church hurt Harvey or Beatrix…I'd be the same way. I'd never forgive the Church either.*

She wondered if Joachim was the type who needed to have an enemy, too. She was about to ask him when she realized he'd disappeared out of sight just as unexpectedly as he'd appeared. His presence really was as thin as a ghost's.

If hostility and anger were the sorts of things that sustained people's existences, what sustained Harvey's existence? Kieli's uneasy gaze roamed the scenery until she found a tall, thin man leaning against the side of a freight car some distance away and lighting a cigarette. Mountain wind tinged with light-gray smoke ruffled his coppery hair.

She was sure that what held Harvey fixed to this world right now was that he needed to do something about the problems in the capital. *So once that's all over…*

"Well, it ain't like I can't understand hostility and anger giving people energy. I mean, regrets and grudges are literally the energy that powers ghosts, after all."

Kieli snapped out of her mood a little bit when she heard the radio say that, and a smile escaped her. The Corporal seemed to not quite be factoring his own existence into that equation.

She was saved by the radio's familiar everyday tones. Its presence with them always gave them positive energy.

"You're powered by complaining, huh, Corporal?" Kieli half-joked, and the radio answered heartily.

"*You got that right! I won't be done for a good million years yet. You two just never quit causing me trouble. You're what people are talking about when they mention 'speaking ill of the dead,' you know! Oh, hey, perfect timing. I've got something to say to you, Kieli.*"

"Huh? Uh, sure."

"*You know I'm always on your side, BUT—*" The radio's tone turned serious all of a sudden, and Kieli's expression turned meek in reaction. When she looked down at it, the radio paused as if to emphasize that it was about to talk about a very grave matter and then said, "*Listen, it's too soon for you to be smooching!*"

"S-sm...?!" *Wait, what generation is that word even from?!* It was all so out of the blue that Kieli was speechless. Paying her no mind, the radio ranted on, sending out stern, grating bursts of static. "*Smooching is something a man and a woman do after they're betrothed to each other! I'll never allow such unchaste behavior while I'm still around to stop it!*"

B-betrothed? Unchaste?! I've never even heard anybody say those words out loud before! "Y-you're out-of-date, Corporal..."

"*There's no such thing as out-of-date in matters like these! Do you hear me, Kieli? You promise me now.*"

"What?! U-um, okay..." Kieli didn't think the radio was being fair, but she ended up overwhelmed by its forcefulness. She sighed, her shoulders drooping. He'd definitely interrupted them at the last moment on purpose back there. She'd *thought* his timing had been too convenient...

The radio was still grumbling to itself like an old geezer from a bygone era. *"I'm telling you, kids these days are ready to just smooch without even thinking about it, not to mention..."*

Heaving a deep sigh, Kieli let her eyes wander from the radio.

She gazed at the old man's back. He was already starting to put up his fourth or fifth new grave marker. It was a broad, strong back, but it looked so solitary. If he hated the Church, why was he making those grave markers? Who did he believe was going to pray over the dead for him?

Kieli quietly lowered her eyes and offered a little moment of silence to the graves that lay beyond the elderly man at work. Kieli didn't know whom she wanted to pray to, either. No god came to mind. But...

Okay then, Corporal, she whispered in her heart, eyes still closed. *Stay around forever. Don't go anywhere, okay? Keep watching over us forever...*

Who did the prayers reach?

Leaning against the side of a freight car, he watched Kieli through his cigarette smoke as she hung her head and was silent, facing away from him. The girl had apparently already doubted God existed before they met two and a half years ago, and yet he sometimes caught her praying anyway, as if she couldn't stand *not* to appeal to someone or something. He was pretty sure even Kieli herself didn't know what she was praying to exactly.

Hey, Harvey, have you noticed that there's no God in the Church?

Now that he thought about it, it might be pretty messed up for a girl in boarding-school clothes who was only fourteen to say something like that.

"She's gotta be an idiot. Why pretend to pray for the sake of something she doesn't even believe in?" said a mocking voice, breaking into his thoughts. When Harvey shot him a sidelong glare, the man in priest's clothes was sitting on the deck of the passenger car with his usual snide smile.

They were about three steps apart. They could go for each other's vital points if they each took one step forward.

"A brat who doesn't believe in the Church's God, related to the Church's highest authority—is that funny or what?" The way Joachim laughed, the sound catching at the back of his throat, seriously got on Harvey's nerves. Since he didn't feel like giving Joachim the pleasure of talking about that, Harvey completely ignored him and asked in a low tone, "What are you going to do after you use Kieli to get near Father Sigri?"

"Don't ask questions you already know the answers to." His tone of voice stayed flippant, without the slightest change.

Harvey kept the same low tone he'd started in, too. "Do you mean to kill him?"

"What if I do? Are you going to stop me?"

Harvey didn't answer right away. It looked as though the old man was done working; he put down his pickax, and Kieli stopped praying, too, and lifted her face. She glanced around searchingly for a moment before she caught sight of them talking together. Her expression turned uneasy, but nonetheless, she pointed toward the front passenger car as if to say *I'll go on ahead*, and started making her way back. Watching her go, Harvey resumed their conversation. "Beatrix is being held at his house."

"Beatrix?" After a blank pause, Joachim said, "Oh! I remember. That loud blonde, right? Oho." To Harvey's annoyance, he repeated that last "oho" several more times before giving another little laugh in his throat, clearly amused about something.

"So those are your terms, then? You're saying if I rescue her, you won't stop me from killing Sigri?"

"...No, I'm not angling for that," Harvey answered. A denial, but as denials went it was a pretty feeble one. It came out in a weak mumble and ended up sounding more as if he was putting off making a real answer than anything else. Now that Joachim had accused Harvey of telling him about Beatrix with that goal in mind, Harvey could see how he might be right, but on the other hand, the man might be a relative of Kieli's. If he were forced to choose between abandoning his old friend or Kieli's relative...no, he didn't want to think about a choice like that right now.

Joachim made an obviously profane noise and spat on the ground.

"There's no reason to hesitate over killing those senile Church fools, and you know it. I don't know whether the guy's Kieli's dad or whatever, but I don't care, either, and there's no way in hell that'll make us even with them after they've had us on the run for eighty years."

"Is getting revenge going to satisfy you? Is there even a point?"

"Point? Why should there have to be a *point* to repaying them for their own hostility? I freaking hate what a disgusting sap you are. Always looking all wise and enlightened all the time—gee, thanks, Mr. Wonderful."

"Fine...So after you make your counterattack against all the hostility you've gotten from people, what are you going to have left? What are you trying to accomplish, ex—"

Skreee—!

The shrill noise effectively ended his sentence for him. Joachim had taken one giant step forward, swinging his right arm...with an open pocketknife in his hand. It left a little scratch where it struck the wall of the freight car, and a few severed red hairs fluttered in the wind.

The air went stiff with tension. After they glared at each other at close range for a bit, standing still, Harvey abruptly pushed Joachim's wrist away with his left hand, and Joachim withdrew and closed his knife without any further fight.

"You never stop pissing me off."

"Don't worry, it's mutual."

Joachim stowed the knife in his pocket, then turned around and jumped up onto the deck and vanished into the train.

Choo...The train sounded its whistle and belched out a thick gust of ash-gray steam. "We're departing. Get on board, please," called the apprentice engineer, leaning out from the movable steps leading up to the locomotive. The old engineer had already finished cleaning up after his work and was wordlessly striding with his pickax past the apprentice and inside.

As Harvey stomped out the butt of his cigarette and began

climbing up to the deck, he suddenly detected a presence at the very edge of his consciousness.

"....?"

He turned around with one foot on the steps. He sensed something move in the shadow of the freight cars behind him. There were about ten of the roofless freight cars packed with brown coal, but as far as Harvey could tell with his still slightly unfocused vision, there wasn't anything particularly out of the ordinary about them. The very last one was blurred from view by a dim mist.

"Harvey?"

Kieli stuck her face out a window in the first passenger car to look for him. No sooner did he grab the railing and haul himself up onto the deck than the train began to pull away from the platform with light vibrations and a heavy billow of smoke. Before he stepped inside, he turned around to take another glance at the line of freight cars behind him, but he didn't see anything especially unusual.

My vision's starting to get worse...

He pressed his hand over his left eye and shook his head a little. The nerves of the left eye he'd been given by the strange-looking beast—Mane—that they'd met in the gorge in the northwestern mining district were hooked up, and it was technically usable, but it was deteriorating faster than he'd thought it would. Sometimes the image there would even cut out for a second. His right eye's sight wasn't completely healed either, so sometimes it were as though he was inside a video screen filled with noise. He needed it to hold out for a while longer.

Harvey took one last look at the line of graves erected along the edge of the platform like a jagged picket fence. They receded from view, and even at this distance they already looked like nothing more than blackened matchsticks stuck haphazardly in an ashtray. He wondered if there was a grave marker for Christoph somewhere in there.

Even though he didn't know where to direct any prayers—for just a second, he closed his eyes and was silent.

When he entered the train through the rear of the second passenger car, Joachim was already gone. Three soldiers turned to look at him from where they'd taken over the front sets of seats on both sides of the aisle to play card games. One of them let his hand slip in panic, and his cards fluttered to the floor in all directions. Harvey ignored it all and kept walking. The soldier who'd bent down to pick up the scattered cards yanked his hand away with a start, although Harvey hadn't intended to deliberately step on him or anything. He was a comparatively young soldier—the one who'd been on watch duty in the front car a little while ago, whose saber he'd borrowed (or stolen).

All the soldiers watched him leave suspended in midmotion, as if they'd been nailed in place. Harvey merely spared them a glance as he walked at his normal pace along the dead center of the aisle. When he reached the forward connecting door, though, he stilled his steps. Apparently, the soldiers had let themselves relax for a moment; when he abruptly turned back to them, they all stiffened again. Harvey imagined he'd hear frightened gulps any second.

He mentally shrugged. Something Joachim said popped into his mind. *Always looking all wise and enlightened all the time*—he didn't think of himself as enlightened one bit, but it was true that while he took issue with Church Soldiers and the Church itself, he'd never particularly felt any hostility or anything. To put it plainly, he didn't see much point in harboring bad will toward people who didn't actually matter to him.

"Is my face scary?" he asked them, jerking his shoulder to indicate the sore on his left cheek. And then there was the bonus fact that his eyes were different colors. No one volunteered to be first to answer, so Harvey narrowed down his targets and focused his eyes on that young soldier squatting in the aisle, who immediately looked flustered.

"K-kind of," the kid blurted.

"'Kind of'?"

He faked a hurt look, and the soldier corrected himself pleadingly: "I...N-no, not really." Harvey didn't think he'd done anything to the kid to make him *that* scared. He lost interest in hearing any more answers. But when he sighed and turned back to face the connecting door, a tentative voice spoke up behind him.

"Um...does that hurt? I heard that Undying soldiers never feel pain..."

On the verge of leaving the train car, Harvey turned around once again. Maybe the soldier thought Harvey was turning to glare; he immediately tried to drop his question. "That is, er, please excuse me."

Bam!

Harvey cut him off by punching the connecting door behind him. The soldier who'd asked him, along with the other two, went pale and froze.

"We're the same."

His voice and the faint vibration of the train wheels echoed through the tense air of the car.

"We're the same as you. When we're injured it hurts, and when something's funny we laugh, and we feel scared sometimes, too, and you know what? We even play cards." He dropped his eyes to the scattered cards on the floor, then raised them again and lifted the corner of his mouth in a tiny smile. "Wanna play sometime? But I'll warn you, I'm good."

"Y-you're on!" the oldest of the soldiers declared vehemently. "No way am I losing to some Undying!" The younger two were clearly rattled, but he accepted Harvey's challenge, face flushed. While this man might still be full of prejudice, he wasn't pointlessly freaking out, either. Satisfied at having finally managed to get someone to respond to him like an equal, Harvey left them with an honest smile.

He stopped for a moment on the deck connecting the first and second passenger cars. The wind lashing and rebounding against the walls of the cars turned turbulent, whipping his hair every which way. He looked up at the patch of sky he could see from between the cars. The same sky hazed with thin, sandy clouds, the sky that hadn't changed on this planet for decades, probably even centuries, was still just floating boundlessly above him the same as ever. It never showed him which way to go next.

Jude…am I at least not too far off course right now…?

At the sight that met his eyes the instant he opened the door to the front passenger car, Harvey was struck with a violent fit of dizziness.

Joachim was squatting in the middle of the aisle with a chocolate bar at his feet, trying to balance what looked like a bucket over it with a stick. It was obviously some kind of mousetrap or something, but Harvey couldn't for the life of him see what Joachim thought he could trap that way... The soldier standing guard next to the connecting door and Kieli, who was sitting in a seat near the middle of the car, were both watching coldly.

"...What are you doing?" he asked with the same cold eyes as Kieli, and Joachim lifted his face without standing up.

"Isn't this how you tamed her and won her over?"

"Like hell, you moron." *How serious is he being?* The scary thing about the way this guy's mind worked was that he might really, actually be serious.

Sullenly clearing away his trap, Joachim whined, "I want a dog, too," in exactly the way a kid would beg for a toy.

"I'm *not* a dog!"

It was when Kieli finally snapped and stood up from her seat to object that it happened.

Owoooo...

A muffled sound very much like a dog's howl echoed somewhere out of sight. Then came several men's voices, not quite wailing but not quite bellowing, and the resounding clash of swords. With a start, Harvey turned back to the deck he'd just come from.

"What's going on?!"

Growing red in the face, the soldier on guard duty dashed out through the connecting door. "Hey, wait—" By the time Harvey'd run out to the deck after him, the guard was already reaching to open the connecting door to the second car.

And then something hit the door's little window with an ugly, wet smack.

No, not "something": the bloody palm of a human hand. The hand slid down the glass and vanished below, leaving behind a sticky bright-red print of all five fingers and the palm. In the same moment, an arm stabbed right through the window, shattering it, and seized the throat of the guard standing frozen in front of the door.

Long, bony, misshapen fingers and green skin, as though the cells had rotted and started melting off—

"Harvey!"

"Don't come out! Stay inside!" he barked back at Kieli automatically, and reached behind him to shut the door to the first passenger car. Cut off by the door, Kieli's voice calling him grew faraway. The moment he hopped onto the second car's deck, he seized the saber of the soldier being held in a choke hold, and—

Shunk.

—plunged it with the full force of his body weight at the window. The unpleasant sensation of his weapon piercing flesh traveled heavily all the way up his arm.

"Ngggnngghhh…"

The low, shaky moan of a beast. The arm sticking out of the door slackened, releasing the soldier, who slumped down onto the deck. The door came loose and skewed outward—along with the saber stuck through it and the *thing* leaning against it on the other side.

Something wrapped in nothing but dirty scraps of cloth. Something that could only be described as a rotting, greenish corpse. Its unfocused eyes rolled around emptily, and then it turned toward him.

That's…

Harvey made a frustrated sound at himself. This was the presence he'd felt before coming inside the train, then. *So it sneaked onto the train while we were stopped…* The saber Harvey'd stabbed it with through the window had gone dead through the center of its carotid artery, but it grabbed the blade of the sword piercing itself with its bare hand, as if that hadn't even slowed it down. Harvey let go of the hilt just in time to avoid getting dragged in close.

"No hard feelings!" he shouted, and with a yell he slammed his shoulder into it with everything he had.

The rush of wind created by the moving train hit the exposed door full-on and blew it clear off its hinges. *Its* giant body was thrown off the deck with it when it went. Harvey almost got thrown off the train right along with them, but at the last moment he managed to cling to the railing. When he turned his head to look over the flapping ends of his coat at them, *it* and the broken door were tumbling end over end into the rock surface along the side of the track. They bounced off and were flung out of sight behind him almost before he could register it all.

Breathing raggedly, he crawled back up over the railing and onto the deck. When he checked on the fallen soldier, the man's cervix was broken; he was already gone.

...For the moment no emotion was coming to him. Maybe his brain wasn't getting enough oxygen.

When he stepped a little unsteadily into the second passenger car, though, it was still too much; he stopped in the doorway and choked back the urge to vomit.

The second passenger car was a sea of bodies and blood. The corpse of the soldier who'd left his handprint on the window of the connecting door lay at his feet. It was the same young soldier he'd been talking with just minutes ago.

The soldier who'd asked *Does that hurt?* in a hesitant voice—whom Harvey'd been *talking with* just a *few minutes* ago.

And the other two—one was lying facedown in a pool of blood in the aisle in front of him. The last one, the man who'd be the oldest, was slumped heavily in his seat. He looked almost as though he were just hanging his head, asleep, but the windowpane next to him was thick with dripping gore. His skull must have been smashed into it.

Simultaneous powerful waves of nausea and dizziness attacked Harvey. He staggered a little, leaning against the door frame and clamping his hand over his mouth. Emotions he didn't really understand started welling up inside him. Anger, regret, maybe even something you could call mourning. While he hadn't felt any hostility toward these people, he hadn't had any particular goodwill either; if anything, he guessed they'd been in midconflict. Still, they were people he'd been talking with just a minute ago—whom he'd talked about playing cards with sometime—who'd tried to act cool and said *No way am I losing to some Undying*—and now their pitiful corpses were lying right in front of him.

If he'd paid attention to that presence he'd felt a little sooner, this wouldn't have happened…

Something creaked. Harvey tensed, straining to sense the slightest presence around him. *There's another one.* A shadowy form darted across his peripheral vision. When he turned around with a start—

Crash!

—the window of the rear connecting door at the other end of the aisle smashed in from the outside.

For the last few minutes she'd been hearing a sort of *scritch-scritch-scritching* against the wall of the train car. "Corporal, there's something out there…!"

"Make sure you don't let go of me, Kieli."

"R-right." Kieli wrapped both arms around the radio and darted her eyes around the train car fearfully. Harvey and the soldier on guard duty hadn't come back since they'd dashed out the rear connecting door.

Kieli thought she heard the sound of something running along the roof directly above her head. When she edged backward, hugging the radio tightly, she bumped into Joachim behind her. She whipped around, reflexively moving away as she did so, only to see Joachim half-shrug at her and actually prop his cheek against the seat back, playing the idle spectator.

"Sounds like we've got a pretty troublesome stowaway on board, huh?" Joachim said, sounding unconcerned, as if it wasn't his problem. Kieli glared daggers at him. Apparently unruffled, he only dropped his head back in disgust and gazed at the ceiling, thinking. "Well, it's not our problem, is it? Why is he putting so much energy into it? Since when is his hobby rescuing people?"

"Harvey's not like you!" As Kieli moved to stomp on his foot, annoyed by the cynical way he'd said that, she heard a loud grating sound coming from outside the train car. She stepped away from him and shrank in on herself, looking around her. *Creak, creak*—as if the entire train car were being throttled.

Where is it? The wall? The roof?

As she looked left and right, trying to sense it, something shot through one of the windows along the side wall, breaking right through the glass. At the sight of the *thing* crawling through the window frame upside down like a spider, Kieli's eyes widened.

Greenish, slack body, two lidless eyeballs that reminded her of an invertebrate's compound eyes, long limbs with the flesh wasted away until the joints stood out unnaturally as it crawled over the window frame and into the train—it really seemed so much like some kind of land crab that Kieli felt a gut-level hatred that made her flesh crawl. She unconsciously took a step back, tripping and hitting her back against the seat on the other side of the aisle as she fell.

A shock wave shot out of the radio in her arms at the same time she stumbled and collapsed into the seat. However, the blast of air missed its mark, only lightly grazing *the thing's* arm before slamming into the wall.

Stretching out its folded limbs like springs, it jumped at her.

Kieli screamed.

As she cringed where she lay sprawled in the seat, it suddenly stopped moving just above her head. When she hesitantly raised her face to look, still covering her head—

"Dammit. Guess I can't let the goose who lays the golden eggs get all banged up, can I?" Joachim griped, as if this was all such a pain in the neck. The folding knife in his right hand was plunged into its chest. It struggled, gurgling painfully, trying to pull out the knife. The more it struggled, though, the farther the knife was pushed in, Joachim's right hand quickly burrowing into its chest. Kieli watched the whole thing with her eyes as round as saucers, frozen in place.

A misshapen stone heart peeked out of the center of *its* chest where the knife had gouged out the flesh. Twitching the corners of his mouth up in a twisted smile, Joachim put even more force behind his right hand and started to pull out the heart. Kieli heard a bizarre creaking sound she couldn't believe could really come from inside a living creature's body.

And Joachim was changing, too. Starting at his right hand around the thing's heart and moving up his arm, his blood vessels bulged out and his skin began to fester and peel. He still wore that warped smile on his cheeks, but the blood vessels bulged out on one of them, too, and the skin there crumbled away until she glimpsed the flesh underneath. Seemingly unfazed by what was happening to his own body, Joachim wrenched off the bio-cables connected to *its* organs and yanked out the heart with his bare hand.

It stumbled back, writhing in what looked like pain, hit the window, and collapsed to the ground like a broken doll. The sight of its lidless eyes vacantly roaming the air as its body twitched fitfully made Kieli feel sick. She clamped both trembling hands over her mouth to hold the vomit in.

After several seconds *it* gradually stopped moving, as if its springs had run down.

Joachim turned to her, still casually holding a clump of biocables and a stone heart dribbling tar-black blood in his right hand. When he wiped his cheek with the back of that same hand, the melted skin peeled right off, and Kieli gave a small shriek. Joachim's right cheek, already starting to regenerate mere seconds later, twisted into a thin smile. "Scared?"

"...I-I'm not scared...!" she answered boldly, though the effect was spoiled by the fact that she was backing away from him, hugging the radio. That was about when the forward and rear connecting doors both flew open at the same time.

"What are you fussing about now?! *This* time I'm throwing you off the train!"

When the elderly engineer came out the forward door brandishing his shovel and saw the state of their car, even he stopped shouting for a moment. Through the rear door, Harvey came back. Kieli's face brightened in relief. Harvey, on the other hand, didn't even spare a glance at what their car looked like. Instead, he slammed the connecting door violently shut and jammed the saber he was carrying through the lever.

Immediately afterward, a green arm broke through the door's little window, its sharp nails clipping Harvey's cheek as he jerked his head out of its path. The door bolted with the saber shook loudly from the outside.

"Get going!" Harvey shouted as he ran toward them, abandoning the door that looked as if it would break any second.

Joachim turned on his heel in a *good grief* sort of way and made a break for it, dashing past the old engineer, who was standing stock-still with his shovel raised overhead, and through the door.

"Kieli, you okay?"

"Y-yeah."

Harvey came up to the seat where she was crashed out in exhaustion. He grabbed her arm and helped her up, and then she started running, too, spurred on by a push at her back.

Just as they made it through the forward connecting door, shoving the old man through it with them, the rear connecting door jerked violently and came loose from the frame to reveal *them.*

Two? No, Three—? Before Kieli's eyes could confirm, she was already across the deck and they were all diving together into the locomotive at the head of the train. "Wh-what the heck is going on?" called the young apprentice, sticking his head out the door suspiciously. He screamed when he saw the monsters in the passenger car behind them.

"Detach us, fast!"

"Wh-what?!" While the apprentice didn't seem to grasp what was going on, at Harvey's order he nevertheless obediently dashed to the coupler connecting the locomotive to the front passenger car and hastily started working the coupling pin. Nervousness made his hands unsteady, though, and he just couldn't seem to get it uncoupled. *They* passed through the passenger car and bore down on them amid all the commotion.

"I'll show you, you damned monsters!"

The one to raise the war cry was the elderly engineer, who

up until then had just been letting them push him along in a stupor. Yelling like a man possessed and brandishing his shovel, he dashed out onto the deck and started swinging it around wildly. "You idiot! Come back!" shouted Harvey, but he paid no mind. One of the monsters grabbed the end of the shovel on the next swing and dragged him into range. The old man disappeared into the passenger car with it.

"Dammit!"

In the same moment that Harvey cursed and started to run out to the deck after him, there was a jolt and a clang as the coupling pin finally lifted.

"Harvey, no!"

Kieli instantly reached out her hand and grabbed the back of Harvey's coat. Harvey turned, stumbling a little, and laid his hand over hers where it clung. "You go on ahead. If I don't catch up to you by the end of the day, head to the capital by yourself. I'll catch up with you later."

"No!" Kieli shouted over him, loudly enough to be heard over the wind screaming through the air all around them.

"Kieli—"

"I don't want to be alone! I won't go! I won't!"

"Go on, just go."

"I don't want to!"

As she yelled, shaking her head, it came home to Kieli just how immature she really was. *No, no, don't leave me alone!*— her fourteen-year-old tantrum-throwing child self was bawling in her mind. She hadn't grown up one little bit since she was fourteen. She was childish, and stubborn, and a tantrum thrower, and all she did was cling to Harvey's coattails wherever they went. But…but she didn't want them to be separated anymore. She kept feeling as if this might be the last time—as if she might never be able to see him again.

"Kieli."

Her clinging hand was forcibly peeled off. Harvey leaned in close to her and started to whisper. The wind blowing on the exposed deck formed a wall of sound around them, and Harvey's low, quiet voice was the only thing she could hear.

"I promise you: I'll come get you no matter what. And then—"

Clang.

There was a hard shock as the cars began to separate, and the last thing he said was half-swallowed by the wind, hard to make out. And then he yelled "Joachim!" and she was shoved back onto the locomotive-side deck and caught by Joachim, who was standing behind her.

"That dolt…! Kieli, please, throw me!" cried the radio's voice through the heaving gusts of wind.

"Stop, please go back! Please!" she shouted, turning to look into the car.

But the apprentice engineer cried back, "That's impossible! And you know what, I don't want to!" before dashing back to the driver's chair.

Kieli turned to face the retreating passenger car one more time. Left on the passenger-side deck, Harvey's face was growing farther away in the blink of an eye.

No. This isn't the same as that time, she told herself. She wasn't the same as she'd been at fourteen. *"Let's take care of all our business,"* that's what Harvey had said. *So come on, Kieli,*

*think about what you have to do, what you should do right now,
and figure it out.*

Pressing her lips tightly together, Kieli gripped the radio's
cord in both hands.

"Harvey!"

He was about to run back into the passenger car when he
heard her call. He stopped and turned around.

"Wait!" And before the word was even out of her mouth, the
radio was flying out of her hands and straight toward him,
screaming, and—*whack.*

It hit him square in the face, and he went blind for a moment.

"Gah! What the hell?!" Harvey shouted, peeling the radio off
his forehead.

"Oh—I-I'm sorry!" Kieli was still leaning out over the edge
of the locomotive's deck in her pitcher's pose, face white as a
sheet.

Behind him, Harvey heard the old man's husky voice cuss-
ing out the monsters. He glanced over his shoulder at the passenger car and grunted in frustration, then turned back
toward the locomotive car one more time, held the radio up in
the air, and gave her a little smile.

To tell her *Thanks. It's okay.* To make sure she knew.

"Joachim! Pull anything funny and I'll kill you!" he spat at
Joachim (who was standing aloof behind Kieli, making a big
show of acting as if the whole thing had nothing to do with
him) in parting, and then he turned on his heel and dived into
the passenger car, hanging the radio around his neck as he ran.

The old man's shovel was lying in the middle of the aisle. As Harvey ran past, he dipped down and picked it up in his left hand. He saw the old geezer himself at the far end of the car, hoisted up by the monster with its talons piercing through his shoulder, *still* showering his opponent with meaningless invective. "Take this!" Letting momentum add to his force, Harvey hit the *thing* attacking the geezer with his shovel as hard as he could.

His enemy tottered back and fell through the doorway out onto the deck, where it was immediately knocked off the train. Its large body tumbled end over end until it was crushed under the wheels. The violent bump and the rasping sound of mincemeat being made sent all the hair on Harvey's body standing on end. With a great shake, one side of the train rocked up into the air.

The force of it made the old man collapse in the aisle. Harvey jogged over and was just kneeling to help him up when a burst of static and a sharp warning came from the radio. *"Herbie! There's another one!"*

Startled, Harvey looked behind him. Immediately afterward, an arm shot out of his peripheral vision and clocked him in the side of the head. He fell over and rolled out onto the deck with the old man in his arms. Once they'd somersaulted a couple of times and crashed into the wall of the car behind them, the rushing wind caught them off balance and they were tossed from the train. Harvey could see the side walls of the cars streaming by right next to him.

Fortunately, cut off from the locomotive, the rest of the train had already slowed down a good bit. Though he'd bounced along the rock face several times, still holding the old man,

and then skidded a pretty good distance with his shoulder scraping hard along the ground, he managed to come to a stop before he rebounded back onto the tracks.

A few seconds after the last of the train cars passed right by his head, the deafening roar of metal scraping hard against rock sounded somewhere up ahead.

"Ugh…"

Harvey gathered his focus and shut off the pain. Then, though he didn't get up, he did somehow work up the energy to lift his head from the ground.

A bunch of the cars in the front had run off the rails and fallen on their sides; the passenger car at the front had stopped just on the verge of going over a ledge. The coal packed in the freight cars was scattered everywhere, and plenty of it was rolling noisily off the cliff.

At the sight of all that disaster in front of him, Harvey heaved a deep sigh. God only knew how many tragic casualties there would have been today if there'd been passengers on board—but fortunately or unfortunately, there weren't any living human beings on that train anymore.

"You alive, Corporal…?"

"Yeah. You?"

"Just barely."

Once he'd confirmed that the radio he'd landed on top of was all right, Harvey propped his hand on the ground and tried to get up, but his sleeve was torn to shreds and he caught glimpses of bone beneath it at his shoulder and elbow. "Damn…" He tried concentrating on the wounds, but he couldn't get the regeneration going at anything faster than a snail's pace. Concentrating all his healing power in one spot gave him a headache and dimmed his sight, so he gave regenerating up as a bad job. He'd blocked out the pain, so there was just a dull tingling sensation all along his left arm.

Harvey looked at the old man on the ground next to him. His back and shoulder were covered in deep claw marks, and blood stained his work clothes. Harvey crawled over and peered at his face, then spoke. "Hey, Gramps, you alive?"

"D-don't touch me...!"

The engineer cursed, if weakly, and slapped Harvey's hand away. "Whoa—" Harvey wasn't exactly steady on his feet himself at the moment; he teetered over and landed lightly on his butt. He ended up just sitting there for a bit, sort of stunned, but the radio angrily piped up, *"Wha—you jerk!"*, so after a beat he realized he'd been rejected. The old man gritted his teeth and stubbornly tried to prop himself up on his own. Harvey could literally see the bloodstains on his work clothes spreading as he watched.

"Come on, don't overdo it."

"I told you not to touch me, you damn Church lapdog!"

He slapped away Harvey's outstretched hand again, but the force of his own blow made his shoulder give out, and he fell back down. Evidently all the pain and blood loss had left him only half-conscious; after that he just lay there facedown on the ground, unable to get up again, breathing shallowly. "Dammit...Sheesh." Harvey clucked his tongue. Then he lifted the geezer's arm to squirm underneath him and tried to load him onto his own back. The radio spat a burst of static in protest.

"Just leave the bullheaded jerk alone! You don't owe him any help after what he said!"

"Oh, shut up…" Apparently he was a bit woozy, too; his hearing was dim and the radio's voice sounded warped to his ears.

"Herbie!"

"I…" Even his own murmuring voice sounded warped. Harvey found himself complaining, half to himself, "I just don't want to regret stuff like this anymore…! Why does it have to happen where I can see it? I want to just leave it alone…" He knew he was getting weirdly pissed, but there it was. The faces of all the people who'd died in front of him because he wasn't able to save them flashed through his mind. It was like that with Christoph. And with those soldiers he'd just shared a casual conversation with, too. *If this crap happened someplace else I didn't care about, I could leave it alone and not care about it! So why do they always die right in front of me? It leaves a bad taste in your mouth when people die right in front of you! You can't just leave it alone then!*

Harvey shouldered the old man and tried to stand up, but his knees crumpled.

"Herbie, stop it!"

"Lay off, I get it…"

"What the hell do you 'get'?! You're going to collapse! Listen to reason for once!"

"I said lay off. You're usually the one…telling me to help… people, so you can't…change your tune…now…"

The radio's increasingly fierce voice grated at his ears. And he was irritated at himself, because even though he knew full well it was saying this stuff out of worry, he still reacted by complaining. *Lay off, lay off,* he chanted over and over in his mind, half at himself. At Harvey, the guy who wanted to leave them alone but couldn't.

When he settled the man on his shoulder one more time and somehow managed to stand up and start walking, something moved in his peripheral vision.

Then there was an unpleasant sensation in his abdomen. He unthinkingly let the geezer he'd finally gotten propped on his back slip off.

He dropped his gaze to his own body to see five sharp claws on gnarled, misshapen fingers sticking out of his side, plunged straight through him from behind. He could see all the way down to the second knuckle. Sinking to one knee with a grunt, Harvey turned to look behind him. A monster half-crushed by the wheels of the train and not much more than a hunk of meat now stretched out an arm to him from where it lay belly-down on the tracks. The damn thing had just jammed its hand through his stomach, and now its empty, pupil-less eyes were looking at him almost pleadingly, for all the world like it was begging him for help...

... Why do everybody and his dog have to die in front of me?

That moment of naive hesitation worked against him. The next thing he felt was the jolt of excruciating pain as it wrenched a chunk of flesh out of his side.

"Bastard!"

A shock wave blasted out of the radio's speaker. It hit the

enemy head-on and sent it flying, but at that same time its arm sliced through the air, and the radio's cord was caught on its nails. The cord snapped, and the radio fell to the ground.

"Corporal!"

When Harvey reached for the radio, reeling from the backlash still, the monster trying to stand up brought its foot down right on top of it. *KKCHK.* The case crumpled, parts flew everywhere, and with one last piercing burst of static like a machine going into the red zone, the sound broke off completely.

"——!"

For a split second Harvey's entire mind fizzled out and went blank.

It lifted one leg for a moment and tilted its head to the side as if it were wondering what it had stepped on. The instant it moved to bring its foot down again, Harvey charged. With a scream of rage, he bore down on the thing; he was hardly able to run through the fire of agony in his side, so it was more of a semicontrolled fall. He knocked it away from the radio with a tackle and then seized the shovel lying next to the track.

He shoved the blade into its back where it lay facedown on the ground and slammed the handle down with all his might. There was the sensation of splitting flesh, and then it banged against something hard. Harvey ignored it, gathering up more energy than he'd known he had left to bring the shovel down even harder.

"Ahhh...hahhh..." He fell to his knees, panting. The shovel slipped out of his hand as he went. A stone heart rolled out of *its* body into the pool of its sticky coal-black blood, dragging a mess of severed cables behind it. With both eyes widened vacantly, the thing abruptly stopped moving.

Harvey's mental circuitry was half-numb. All he felt was nausea.

"Corporal…" he called in a scratchy voice as he crawled over to the radio, scraping his knees along the ground. Its case was crushed horribly out of shape. There was no answer. "Corp'ral…" Even Harvey heard how incredibly pathetic he sounded. *Why was the last thing I said to him "lay off"? Not like that… I don't want it to end like that.*

"I'm sorry, I'm sorry… Please, answer me…"

He dragged himself the last few inches and crouched over the radio, pressing his forehead down into the dirt, prostrating himself, and pleaded. But no matter how many times Harvey called him, not even the feeblest answering static came from the speaker.

He sensed a presence above him. He didn't have the mental or physical strength left to lift his head anymore, but after a little while he did sluggishly roll his eyes up to look anyway. Farther along the tracks at the edges of his blurred vision, several rotting, greenish corpses were crawling out of the overturned train.

"Nggnnghhh…"

"Nng…ng…"

The pained-sounding groans of the literally undead echoed down the mountain railroad on the moaning wind.

One by one, the corpses pushed themselves up into a slouch and half-walked, half-drifted like ghosts toward the first prey they saw—in other words, *this way.* "Damn…it…" Cradling the radio with his arm, Harvey turned to the engineer, but even in his own mind he seriously doubted that he still had enough strength left to shoulder the old man and run. He tried to stand up and his foot slipped. He fell to his knees.

Just then—

Whump!

The sound of a thick gunshot like a blast of heavy compressed air rang out.

A hole opened up in the body of the corpse leading the attack, and it fell flat on its face. More shots, a whole series of gunshots rang out, and one by one the corpses were blown away, collapsing to the ground like useless broken dolls.

Don't tell me—

Still crouching on the ground, Harvey raised his head and squinted down the track.

The track itself was wavering in the haze created by the shimmers of heat in the air, but far along it he made out a group of human forms. Forms in clunky full-faced armored robes, pure-white ones that stood out against the jet-black muzzles of the big-bore rifles they all carried—

A pack of grim reapers in monochrome.

CHAPTER 2
CONCRETE GUM TASTES LIKE CATS

So bored.

The tedium was seriously starting to test his limits, so he decided to tease the cat.

"Want some gum? You know, gum." He crouched down in one corner of the platform and tried holding out his gum toward the scruffy-looking animal watching him from where it lay curled up next to the station house wall. It came up to him slowly, looking wary, but just before it got close enough for him to capture it, it tensed up and started to dash away, so he grabbed it by a hind leg.

"Greeoww!"

With a thick screech, it clawed hard at his hand, causing him to reflexively let go. Suddenly free, the cat's excess momentum sent it into an undignified somersault before it tore off like a bat out of hell straight up the wall and around behind the station house, one last menacing growl echoing after it. "Dammit. And here I was going to give it some gum, too." He'd figured it might kill some time to get gum all over the cat and watch it spaz out.

Since he didn't have anywhere else to put it anymore, he tossed the gum in his mouth and chewed it noisily, looking down at the back of his hand where he'd been attacked. The blood seeping out of the three puckered scratches gradually transformed into something like black coal tar that oozed like pus, and the regeneration began. Soon the repairs had gone too far, and the clumps of extra cells rotted and fell to his feet, where they immediately shriveled up, their moisture evaporating. He watched them for a while, but eventually he lost interest.

Without lifting himself out of his crouch, he turned his head and purred "Hey" in a coaxing voice. The girl sitting at the edge of the platform kept her eyes fixed on the point where the track disappeared over the horizon and didn't answer.

"Hey. Hey."

No response.

"Come on, *hey*. Let's give up and go already. He won't show up even if we wait here till Doomsday. He got eaten, okay?"

Going that far finally got him a response. She looked his way once, expression tight, before turning primly back around to face front again the next moment.

"You can go wherever you want, all by yourself. Nobody asked you to wait here with me."

Wow. Now that's a seriously different attitude than she takes with Ephraim. Joachim shrugged his shoulders, wondering if she really hated him that much. "But I can't get in to see Father Sigri unless I'm with you. It would waste the whole beautiful story line of my earning his eternal gratitude by protecting his daughter from an attacking pack of monsters and returning her safely to him." When he looked down at his hand again as he spoke, the wounds had opened up again like the gaping mouths of carnivorous plants, and more pus was oozing out. He licked one of them. The tastes of coal-tar blood and festering cells mingled with the gum in his mouth.

When he happened to lift his eyes, Kieli had turned to look at him again.

"When you see this...Father Sigri person, what will you do?" Her voice was grim. "Will you kill him?"

"What if I do? Are you going to stop me?" he asked, just as he'd asked Ephraim. Kieli glared at him with narrowed eyes for a few moments, but then she resumed looking forward, answering, "Nah."

After that, she didn't say another word. She gazed down the track again, posture clearly broadcasting that she wouldn't budge an inch. There she was on the very edge of a deserted train platform that saw only freight cars. Sandy heat shimmers flickered on the horizon where the tracks cutting straight through the wilderness vanished, and the sky there gradually took on the copper hues of evening. The sun would set before long.

"Sheesh. I'm gonna take a walk or something." Joachim got to his feet, sighing. When he stood up, the rotten flesh crumbled from his right hand to dribble down to the ground in front of him. He clicked his tongue in irritation and shoved the hand into the pocket of his greatcoat.

Kieli thought she caught a glimpse of a human form down the tracks, and anticipation had her starting to stand up for a moment before she realized that it was an illusion created by the early-spring heat. She sat back down dejectedly on the edge of the platform, hugging her knees.

The locomotive car—all that was left of their train—was parked at this empty station, where there was no one in sight. The young apprentice engineer had apparently gone to call someone for help. She'd seen him run into the station house some time ago, but he hadn't come back.

He'd told her on the way that this place was only ever used for unloading the freight trains that ran between the mine shafts along the mountain range or for collecting or dropping off workers for those mine shafts. It was a cheerless sight, with nothing to it but a ramshackle station house made of galvanized iron. This station had probably been livelier back when the northwestern mining district had prospered as the store of the capital's resources, but now there weren't any workers, let alone travelers. It was deserted. Behind it was a squalid, cramped slum clinging to the slope of the mountain that she assumed was the settlement the workers used to live in. She'd heard the whole area around here was a collection of slums for the people who couldn't live in the capital even though they were providing labor for the capital. Evidently the waterways connecting the mountain range and Gate Town sprawled out underground here, too; the whole place smelled like old water.

Mixed in with the smell of water, the emotions of the people who'd once passed through here hovered faintly.

Train stations were places that tended to accumulate lots of people's emotions. Excitement at arriving in a new town, feelings of people who'd had to leave someone precious behind, regret at not being able to go somewhere else even if they wanted to, feelings of people who'd waited and waited for someone who never came home…

Beyond the dense huddle of low buildings in the slum towered the town wall—the gate to the capital. Through that gate was the "mechanical city." On the far side she could see the city skyline: a forest of dark-gray steeples rising above the wall. To the pilgrims who set out for Church headquarters as the final destination of their pilgrimage, that cluster of towers must inspire awe and respect; Kieli looked at the heavy sky gray with gas and thought it mostly looked gloomy. Just like a cluster of grave markers.

Whose grave markers...?

Please don't let them become the graves of the people I love.

When *that* thought popped into her mind, Kieli put a hand to her heart and pressed hard. *Harvey, Corporal...are you okay? Where are you now...?*

She tried to hold back her uneasiness as best she could. To keep herself from thinking about upsetting things, she just called up Harvey's words in her mind over and over.

You know that house by the Easterbury transfer station, where Tadai lived?

It's pretty run-down right now, but I think I want to fix it up and live there.

The careless tone he used was just his usual habit; her heart soaked up the low voice speaking those words quietly and mildly to her, and she started to feel calmer.

Meow, something at her feet whined suddenly. Kieli looked down and blinked.

Beneath where she sat with her legs stretched out on the platform—cats. And not just a couple; there were four or five of them, some white and some black and some striped. They milled around at her feet, occasionally jumping up onto the platform.

"Wh-what do you...want...?" she asked the cats without thinking, though she cringed a little as she spoke.

All of them looked like strays, skinny and covered in dirt. Come to think of it, now she remembered seeing a cat or two when they'd first arrived at this station, too. The apprentice engineer had explained to her that stray cats gathered in this neighborhood, apparently because someone was feeding them. Which was fine, but did stray cats usually come up to strangers so unguardedly like this?

Then she realized that they *weren't* coming up to her; there was another person sitting next to her—although she was sure there hadn't been anyone there a moment ago. A little startled, Kieli turned to look. A man in whitish work clothes sat on the edge of the platform beside her, nonchalantly looking down at the cats by their feet.

She was openly staring at him, completely forgetting her manners, when he turned his head in her direction. When his eyes met Kieli's, he looked a little surprised, too. But then he quickly gave her a faint smile and said, "Hello."

The greeting was calm and so natural that Kieli responded "H-hello" in kind. He was a skinny young man with a kind-looking smile. She wondered if the work clothes meant he was a laborer at the mine shaft.

The cats had all been gathering around him, not Kieli. They prowled around his legs and rubbed their heads against him, or came up to him and sat down, looking perfectly at ease there as they scratched one ear with a hind leg. Catching Kieli looking on wonderingly, the man smiled wryly and said, "I gave them a little food a while back, and they just sort of all gathered here."

Kieli nodded vaguely. "Right…" So he was the one who'd been feeding the cats.

But...

As if he'd read her mind, he cast his eyes downward, too, looking lonely.

"I can't feed them anymore, though...Go on, I told you; I don't have anything." He shook his leg at them, gesturing for them to go away, but the cats moved in closer, unconcerned, and looked up at him expectantly.

Kieli thought for a minute, then dragged her bag up onto her lap and rooted around inside until she dug out a packet of jerky she'd packed to eat on the road. She tore some little pieces off and scattered them at her feet. The cats looked up at her with guarded eyes. But then when the biggest white cat came up and bit into the jerky, the other cats followed. The smallest cat, a skinny black one, hung back warily long after all the others, but eventually it slowly came in closer as though it couldn't stop itself anymore, popping its head out from between the other cats to begin eating greedily. Apparently they were all hungry.

After watching the cats for a while, the man smiled at her. "Thank you."

"It's nothing." Kieli smiled shyly back. "The cats are really attached to you, aren't they?" she said with another smile as they watched the cats nibble at the jerky. But the smile he gave her in return seemed troubled.

"I gave them some leftovers once just on a whim; I wasn't really planning on looking after them forever...I don't know why they got so attached to me." He sighed heavily.

Something about his grumbling gave her déjà vu. She'd seen

that expression a lot, once upon a time. Who was it? He reminded her of someone.

Oh—Harvey…

She realized before long that she'd connected him mentally with the way Harvey'd been when they first met.

In the beginning, he'd looked really put out that some nuisance of a girl he'd only ever talked to on a whim had gotten attached to him and started following him everywhere. Still, he never had chucked her aside in the end… Which made this littlest black cat her fourteen-year-old self, she guessed. The way it was black, and tiny, and unsocial sort of reminded her of her old self.

She and the man watched the cats side by side for a while longer. It was a quiet interval, just the two of them and the cats, as the sandy sky gradually darkened with the approaching dusk. The faint sound of boilers running permeated the air: a low noise like a rumbling of the ground that came day and night from the mechanical city towering behind them.

When they eventually polished off all the jerky, the cats crowded around the man's feet again and started playing. They didn't show any signs of gratitude toward Kieli. The man swung his legs at them a little harshly and said, "I'm telling you, I can't look after you anymore. Just go somewhere else already. Go on, go away."

He tried to shoo them off, but the cats seemed to think he was playing with them; they were happily jumping away and then jumping back again, trying to pounce at his legs. That little black one managed a good pounce, but it slid right through the man's leg and splatted on the ground. Then it got back up and looked around, confused.

The cats...probably didn't understand.

They didn't know he wasn't here in this world anymore. They didn't know he was just one of the lingering thoughts from all kinds of people floating around the station.

"Why won't you go...? It doesn't have to be me, right? There are other people who'll give you food."

He hung his head and sighed in defeat. Kieli couldn't help laughing a little. When he shot her a reproachful look, she hastily apologized and changed the subject.

"Um, I was just thinking that they really like you."

"If I hadn't been the one to feed them first, they would have been fine with someone else."

"But you *were* the one to feed them."

The man blinked at Kieli's answer, as if he hadn't expected that. Kieli herself was a little surprised to hear the words come out of her mouth. She thought through what she meant as she continued. "...Maybe you're right, and someone else would have done. Maybe it would have been the same with anyone else. But you were the one who showed up that day, so you were the one they decided they liked." Kieli paused. "Does it have to be more than that?"

For a few seconds he gazed at her open-mouthed, and all of a sudden Kieli was embarrassed that she'd kind of made a speech at him. "Um, I guess that's...obvious, huh..." She trailed off and shrank away nervously. The man kept on gazing, the cats still playing with his legs, but eventually his expression thawed and his thin face broke into a soft smile.

"You're right…It is obvious, but I guess that kind of thing is all it takes to spark a relationship when you get right down to it, huh?"

Kieli felt her heart seize up in the face of that smile from someone who reminded her of Harvey, and she lowered her eyes. At which point she realized that the cats were starting to play around her feet, too, as if perhaps they'd finally decided to acknowledge that she'd given them the jerky. Happy, she looked up and said, "Oh! They're getting attached to me, too—"

—but the man had already disappeared.

Kieli and the stray cats were the only ones left on the platform. The early-spring northern winds blew around them, still chilly, yet also strangely comfortable, like a parting smile.

After gazing for a while at the place where he'd been, Kieli turned her eyes back toward the tracks.

It felt as though she was the same as the homeless cats and the spirits lingering here waiting for something.

It was only a tiny coincidence that had sparked that fourteen-year-old girl like a scruffy, orphaned black cat to join an Undying man and a radio-possessing ghost on their journey. Without that chance meeting, she might have been living out a totally different future right now. She might have still been living a humdrum life at the boarding school in Easterbury. Maybe she would have met someone else and gone on a different journey. Maybe that other person would have become someone special to her.

Maybe things would have been the same with anyone else who'd set off that first coincidence, as long as they got her out of that suffocating boarding school.

Now, though, it was too late: nobody else would do. Somewhere along the way the people she'd met had become special, had come to mean the world to her, had come to be people she wanted to protect at any cost, even though there probably wasn't one specific moment she could point to when the switch had flipped and *anyones* had become *someones* that she wouldn't want to trade for anyone else.

The man's words sprang back to life in the back of Kieli's mind: *I guess that kind of thing is all it takes to spark a relationship.*

Maybe I should go back to look for him . . .

She'd sat all by herself with her hands wrapped around her knees in a deserted station like this once before. That time it had been a dog beside her, she remembered, instead of cats. And a man had been there to tell her *Then you can just go look for him* and give her a push in the right direction. An old station manager who looked at home in his dark-green uniform and cap. He'd said that waiting was the only thing he could do anymore, but that she had the legs to walk on her own.

Maybe I should go back to look for him, she thought again. But . . .

I promise you: I'll come get you no matter what. And then—

And then. What had Harvey said at the very end? She called up the memory of the words she'd just barely heard before the wind carried his voice away.

And then.
Let's all go home together.

❧

He wasn't sure who'd told him way back when that he should kill as many enemies as he could; that person from his very first memory wore a blank, featureless face in his mind, and he couldn't recall it into focus. But he killed a bunch of them as he was told, and for whatever reason it got him compliments, so he killed even more. He was fairly proud of the fact that he killed more than anybody else.

"Not enough yet…" He scraped the caked blood and fat of the enemy off his saber with a finger and licked it. He'd killed fewer people than usual that day, and he was in a bad mood. It still shouldn't have changed the fact that he'd killed the most, but later he'd heard there was someone who'd killed even more than him. He wondered what the guy was like. A big, dumb, savage oaf?

While he was standing there licking blood off his saber and thinking, a truck came straight at him from one side out of nowhere, engine roaring, and…he was sent flying.

He landed on his ass. As the stunned members of his unit circled around him at a careful distance, Joachim raised his eyes to look up, equally stunned. The truck had veered off in a seemingly random direction, sending up a cloud of dust until it finally came to a stop and the broad-shouldered form of their superior climbed a bit unsteadily down from the passenger seat.

"Never drive again, Ephraim," Joachim could hear the man saying.

And then *he* climbed out of the driver's seat. He tilted his head to the side, still expressionless, and said, "I hit something."

"...Yeah, *me*," Joachim announced, and stood. The newcomer turned to face him. He seemed pretty damn uninterested for someone who'd just almost killed Joachim.

His first meeting with that red-eyed, red-haired bastard sucked right from his first impression.

The coughing started again.

Crumpling to his knees by the back wall of the station house, Joachim hacked up the substance forcing its way up his throat, and his gum along with it. Dark organ meat twined around gum and fell in one mass just in front of his knees, where it writhed like a living creature for a while before it shriveled up. As he pressed his forehead into the wall and rode out the discomfort, he gripped a few pebble-sized hunks of concrete on the ground with his right hand. They scraped together noisily in his fist and bit into his steadily rotting palm.

Still clenching the concrete fragments, he put his fist in his mouth and gnawed on the skin. The putrid skin tore off as if it was nothing. He crunched the flesh of his hand and the concrete fragments with his back teeth.

He abruptly came back to himself when he heard one of his molars crack, and spat out the meat and concrete.

"Damn it..."

Joachim collapsed to the ground, scraping his forehead against the wall as he went. The tastes of concrete and blood soaked his mouth. They did nothing to neutralize the unpleasantness of the taste of vomit and excrement—they heightened it, in fact.

These occasional fits of cell decay and excessive regeneration had started happening more and more often. At the same time he vomited out rotten pieces of his organs, his consciousness dimmed; when he came to, there he was doing crazy things like eating his own flesh.

The right hand he'd balled into a fist was shaking slightly.

Am I scared? Me? Of what? That I might eat myself someday? Or of death itself?

He felt royally pissed off at himself. If his only other option was letting a monster take over his mind, the thing to do was to rip his own heart out first; that was all. *Right this minute—*

Joachim put a hand to the center of his chest and grabbed hard. All five fingers dug into his skin, and blood seeped out.

Then he heard the smacking sound of someone eating something.

Still on his hands and knees against the wall, he turned his cheek along the brick to look. A dirty, scruffy cat was sniffing at the organs he'd thrown up and setting about eating them. It was the same cat who'd run away earlier when he'd tried to lure it with gum: a black-and-white tabby with its half-chopped-off tail standing at attention.

"...You're gonna make yourself sick, you know," Joachim warned it, for what that was worth, but the tabby cat must have been really hungry, because it kept right on eating the rotten meat without showing the slightest sign of listening to him (not that he knew whether it could understand human words or not). After gazing at the tabby cat's stubbed tail a little fuzzily for a while, he asked, "Wanna eat this? It's fresher."

He tried holding out his right hand without getting up from the ground. In the wounds on his palm where it'd been pierced by the concrete shards, he could glimpse fresh meat that was only just beginning to regenerate. The tabby lifted its head from the rotten meat and turned to face him, but then caution froze it as perfectly still as a piece of furniture.

"Relax. I'm not gonna bite you. Probably."

When he made a little beckoning gesture with his right hand, it slowly walked toward him with silent feline steps, licked at the blood on his palm, and began eating. Apparently it was pretty well starved. Enough to eat rotted human flesh. "Hungry, huh? Oh…" he muttered vaguely. The tabby was preying on his meat with a passion. Joachim wouldn't be surprised if it got indigestion or some weird disease from this, but he figured it had only two choices either way: die on a full stomach of whatever contagions he was carrying, or continue starving to death. "That tickles…"

He'd shut down his sense of pain, so the sensation of the cat eating the flesh of his palm didn't hurt, but its tongue gave him a crawly feeling. After a while the tabby seemed to have satisfied its hunger for the time being, and it stopped eating and began licking at the blood on his palm.

"Come over here."

He tried stretching his other hand toward the tabby. It lifted its head and gave him a measuring look. He thought it might run, but instead it slowly drew closer, pushing its neck up into his extended left hand. The grubby stray's fur was matted and stiff, and a good portion of it was missing.

Joachim sure as hell didn't know how to pet a cat, but when he gave its throat an experimental tickle, the tabby made a sort of purring noise. "Feel good?" he asked. It purred again. His cheek, pressed against the ground, quirked up in a smile without warning. *Huh, so cats purr when you do stuff like this?* It was the first time he'd ever petted one, so he'd never known. *This is kind of entertaining. A little more entertaining than playing around sticking gum on it.*

Stroking the cat's throat with his fingertips, he thought distractedly, *I wonder if it's edible.*

It's so starved, its muscles are probably too stringy. Probably wouldn't taste any good.

My mouth would get all full of hair, too, unless I pulled it all off first.

Seems like it'd be hard to eat…

Suddenly he heard a rumbling coming from somewhere. The tabby cat he was just now finally starting to tame sprang back, scaled the wall again before he could blink, and disappeared.

Joachim realized it was the rumble of approaching wheels. Low, rhythmic reverberations.

What…?

Half-sitting up, Joachim suddenly realized something, and shuddered at himself.

He turned back to look in the direction the tabby cat had darted off in.

Wait, who was in charge of my thoughts just now? Was it me?
Who was it?

Joachim put a hand to his temple. His thoughts were fuzzy, and there was a dull pain deep inside his skull.

The sound of wheels came closer. He stood up with one hand against the wall for balance and went around to the front of the station house, where Kieli was standing on tiptoe at the edge of the platform, squinting down the track. From across the wilderness growing tinted with dusk, he could see a train car approaching in the distance. An armored train car, painted black—*No way that overdone, gratuitously extravagant armor belongs to the normal Security Forces. They must be Undying Hunters.*

"Hey—you idiot!"

Kieli was just standing there on the platform, so he grabbed her arm and yanked her back next to the station house with him. He was still unsteady, though, and he ended up on his rear end next to the wall with his arm sort of around her stomach. "Hey, let me go!" Kieli kicked her legs and struggled to get free. Then she noticed Joachim's arms around her were rotting and gave a little shriek, squirming and flailing even harder. "L-let go of me!"

But when he whispered into her ear, "It's the Undying Hunters," still holding her from behind, she seemed to understand. She stopped struggling.

As the two of them watched with bated breath from the shadows, the armored train car clattered up to the platform with four times the awful roar of a normal one, coming to a halt with a burst of white steam.

They saw the apprentice engineer sprint out of the station house shrieking about something. A stretcher with a patient on it was lowered out of the armored car. It was that old fool of an engineer. He looked badly hurt, with blood oozing thickly out of the first-aid bandaging they'd given him, but apparently he'd managed to not get eaten by the monsters. Joachim was a little disappointed. That geezer had been such a pain in the neck, yelling at them all the time, that he wouldn't have minded the guy becoming monster food.

Eyes frozen on the armored car, Kieli croaked, "What about Harvey...?"

"Looks like he's not there. Guess he got eaten, or maybe they killed him?"

Kieli turned on him with a glare. Then she suddenly wriggled, trying to make a break for it, so he grabbed her torso harder and reined her in again—"Come on, wait!"—which naturally meant they wound up falling down in a heap again.

"Hey, hey, are you stupid? What's the point of going over there? Are you just going to walk up and blurt, 'Did you see an Undying on your way here?' "

"......"

Kieli bit her lip and fell silent, glaring at the ground as though it were her mortal enemy. The hands she'd balled into fists were shaking slightly. She forcibly shook off Joachim's restraining arms and stood up, but instead of dashing away, she stood in place and stared at the armored car from the shadow of the wall. After a brief conversation with the apprentice engineer, the soldiers who'd unloaded the stretcher went back inside, and the armored car rumbled off somewhere in a clamor of unnecessarily overbearing clanging and banging noises.

After it was out of sight, Kieli dashed out of the shadows and over to the apprentice engineer, who was loading the stretcher into the parked locomotive.

"What about Harvey? What happened to him?!" Joachim heard her ask the old man on the stretcher eagerly. But the old man seemed to be unconscious. No answer came. When Kieli just stood there, the apprentice asked her, "I'm going to go one more station farther and take him to the hospital there. What do you want to do?" as he pushed the stretcher up the rest of the way into the locomotive.

"...I'm going to wait a little longer," Kieli answered in a dark voice, and Joachim saw her shake her head. The apprentice only said, "Okay."

Once the train that was down to just one car pulled out of the station in a cloud of steam, she went back to standing on the edge of the again deserted platform and began gazing down the track.

Oh, come on, we're going to wait even longer?

She showed no signs of ever budging an inch. Wishing she'd just give it a rest already, Joachim sat down with his back against the station house wall. The copper-stained evening sun was hanging about halfway above the horizon beyond the train tracks. When its outline sank completely below the horizon, it would be night.

As the sunlight grew dim, the smell of water seeping out of

the aqueducts began to thicken. There were lots of exit points around here for the underground waterways coming from the mountains. He didn't know for sure whether *they* were nocturnal or not, but he wouldn't put it past them to crawl out of there under cover of night.

The evening sun was steadily swallowed up by the horizon until the girl standing alone was backlit, a silhouette trimmed in burnt orange. Just before the last rays of light disappeared, the whole horizon was dyed with copper-red light; when the rays finally sank away completely, that line of light steadily vanished, too, eaten away by the slate-blue of night encroaching at either end.

Without warning, the girl who'd faded to a shadow that blended into the evening darkness whirled around to face him.

Joachim blinked, puzzled. He'd been resigning himself to waiting here against the wall a good while longer.

"I'm going to the capital," she declared in a hard voice.

"Given up, then? Admitted he got eaten after all?" he asked sardonically, grinning, but Kieli didn't rise to the bait. She just answered crisply, "Harvey told me to go on ahead if he didn't make it by the end of the day. He promised to come get me no matter what. So I'm going to go on ahead…and take care of what I need to take care of."

Her voice didn't even waver. As Joachim watched in silence, a little daunted, Kieli resettled her bag on her shoulder and started walking quickly away.

She looked as though she was keeping up that plucky attitude, but when she walked past him, her tightly clenched fists were trembling slightly. It was obvious she was desperately forcing that hard look on her face. Joachim mentally shrugged in disbelief. *Sigh... I'm damned if I can see why she'd try so desperately to believe in that guy. Is he really worth getting that obsessed with?*

Kieli's steps paused for a moment, cutting off that train of thought. She turned back to look at him where he still sat watching her go.

"Aren't you coming? You want to use me, right?"

"Eh... Sure I'm going," Joachim answered carelessly, but Kieli's eyebrows drew together when she saw that he didn't actually try to get up.

"Can't you stand?"

"Nope. Truth is I can't. Help me up."

"......"

He gave Kieli a cool-as-a-cucumber grin. She turned back around again with an openly revolted expression on her face, and started walking off without him. *Sheesh, she has no sense of humor.* Whenever he tried to tame her, win her over, she ended up coldheartedly deserting him. Joachim swore under his breath. She reminded him of that damn tabby cat. Watching the girl leave out of his peripheral vision, he sank his head back against the wall and looked up.

The sky was that gloomy blue-gray of nightfall. It looked the same color as his own eyes.

He pondered what the difference could have been between him and that guy. He was fairly sure they'd stood at pretty much the same starting line in the beginning. *We both become*

Undying, and we killed about the same number of people, too, and we both wandered through life for eighty years after we failed to die in the War—but somewhere along the way someone showed up to reach out a hand to him, and even though I'm pretty sure there was all kinds of stuff I wanted, it all slipped through my fingers in the end.

What happened to make our paths split so far apart? When did it happen?

If I'd been the one to meet her first, would she have reached out a hand to me?...Nah, probably not, he thought masochistically.

And then something long and thin was reached out to him, right before his eyes.

At some point while he'd been lost in thought Kieli had come back, and she was currently scowling and thrusting a stick she must have picked up somewhere toward him. When Joachim blankly grasped the end of the stick, she tugged with both hands to help him stand up. As soon as he was upright, she tossed it away and wiped her hands off on the hem of her coat as though she'd touched something dirty. *Talk about being treated like dirt.*

"I don't know how to get to the capital," she said coolly. "It would be very inconvenient if you didn't take me there." By the time she'd finished delivering this parting shot, she'd already turned on her heel and started walking.

"...Allow me to accompany you, miss," Joachim called after her, snickering at her rapidly retreating back.

Before he started out after the girl, he turned back to look at the platform one more time. The train tracks cut straight across the darkening wilderness toward the horizon.

*　　*　　*

What made our paths split off in different directions? Where did I step wrong?
If I didn't step off the path, I—

He abruptly turned his back on the tracks.

Stepping on his own long, faint shadow against the concrete, he started walking.

CHAPTER 3

"LIKE MOTHER, LIKE DAUGHTER."

Hey, what color is God? Julius had once asked his nursemaid. As a small child he'd had an endless need to know things; he wouldn't rest until he'd cleared up whatever question was bothering him.

Well, young master, color is essentially light. God is light itself. He holds all colors within him, so He doesn't have one particular color He has to be.

That was more or less how her answer went, he remembered. At the time he'd been totally awestricken, and he'd accepted the answer without question, but thinking back on it now that he knew something about the principles of color, wouldn't mixing all colors together make Him virtually black? It would mean God was black, a jet-black that swallowed up the light.

This is a silly argument...

Gazing down at the dark-gray city below him, Julius sighed and left off thinking about stupid things. The view from the windows of his family home was a steel city that looked almost like a great collection of steam locomotives, making extravagant use of the scant mineral dregs that could still be gotten from the mining district to the northwest. Thick smog belched unendingly from the exhaust pipes sticking out of every corner of every building. If you looked down on them from this mansion near central headquarters, the ordinary residential districts in the middle and lower strata looked like gray miniature gardens dim with smog.

He heard one of the servants say "Welcome home, sir," and things got noisy down on the first floor. He turned away from the window on the landing halfway up their staircase that he'd been gazing at the skyline through and jogged down the steps. He could see his father in the entryway, surrounded by servants. Julius had been waiting ever since he'd heard that his father would be able to make it home today.

"Dad."

"Ah, Julius. Did you get taller again?" his father said as soon as he saw him, taking off his greatcoat and handing it to one of the servants. "I was hoping we could have dinner together, but it turns out I have to go right back to the station. I'm only stopping by here."

Julius was privately dismayed. He didn't let it show, though. Shoving it down, he said, "Oh, I see . . . that must be rough." He was relieved that he'd managed to answer with something that sounded understanding. But still, their schedules hadn't overlapped once over the whole end-of-semester vacation, and now look what happened just when they finally got to see each other for the first time in a month . . .

He couldn't just whine like a spoiled kid about it, though. Strings of disturbances were happening both in the upper stratus of the capital and on the streets of the ordinary residential districts lately, and the Security Forces were saddled with a whole mess of thorny problems at once. They'd been juggling madly just to keep all the balls in the air. His dad had his hands fuller than ever, to the point where Julius worried he might actually work himself to death.

"Is there anything I can help out with?"

"Thanks for the offer, but it's not so bad that we need to bring you in yet." He flashed Julius a cheerful smile, but his cheeks were a little pale with exhaustion. He might only be of medium height, but he'd always been relatively well-built.

Now Julius thought he'd gotten a little thin—maybe "haggard" would be a better word, even. "Sorry I don't have much time to talk. You're going back tomorrow, is that right?"

"Yeah."

The spring semester started in two days, so Julius had planned to go back to the seminary school dormitory tomorrow. The seminary was plenty close enough for him to commute from here, but his busy father was hardly ever at home and had thought it would be better for his son to live with friends than all alone with the servants, so Julius was living in the dorms on his advice. Not that he actually had all that many "friends," really.

One of the problems causing a stir in the capital these days was a string of the same sort of monster incidents that had happened before in "Gate Town." The monsters were showing up in the capital's ordinary residential districts and on the streets of Gate Town, among other places, and there had been a rash of attacks on citizens over the last month or two.

"There was another incident today, so we're stepping up security even more. It seems like there have been a lot of victims down in the lowest areas in particular, where the exits of the waterways are...I don't want you going outside without being careful either, you hear me? It's dangerous."

"Have you found out what they are, Dad?"

His father's face clouded evasively at his question. Even though his dad was a tough nut to crack, and Julius had the feeling it would be many years yet before he got any good at dragging his real thoughts out of him, his dad didn't tell lies. Julius was fairly certain he had a good idea what was going on, but from this reaction, he guessed it wasn't the kind of idea his dad could make public. Something that couldn't be made public... Which meant there was someone out there it would make trouble for if it went public. Someone at the top, most likely.

Trouble was threatening the upper ranks of the Church from inside and out right now; a weird disquiet had been hanging in the air for months. The people who were supposed to be wreathed in light, the objects of Julius's faith for the past sixteen years, seemed to be languishing in the same murky gray as the city itself.

Something appeared to strike his father, who'd been stroking his chin, pondering something. "Come to think of it, Julius," he said, "there's a little something I'd like you to do for me after all. Will you do me a favor?"

"Huh? Sure, what is it?" Julius asked quickly, leaning forward. He'd always wanted to become someone who could really be useful, but this was the first time in his life that his father had ever asked him for a favor. Before he knew it, his eyes were shining with excitement.

"Two things, actually. First, I'd like you to go visit a certain girl."

"Girl?" *Well, that's not what I was expecting.* He couldn't help feeling disappointed. This mission seemed kind of lame. He'd been just a little bit hopeful it would be a job more like fighting the monsters or investigating them or something... His father chuckled good-naturedly, clearly reading his mind. It felt as though he was seeing right through Julius and thinking he hadn't changed since he was a little boy who liked to go on imaginary adventures. Completely embarrassing.

"Now, don't be like that. The second job is close to what you want. And while you're doing *that* one, I just want you to go check on a friend's daughter who's about to arrive in the capital. I haven't gotten word from my men, but if everything's going to plan, she should get here today or tomorrow."

"Huh," Julius said disinterestedly. Even after hearing the explanation, he just couldn't really get into it.

"She's just about your age, you know. Look."

Half of Julius's mind was occupied with thinking *I hope the second job is something about the monsters* as he took the photograph his dad was holding out to him and casually looked down at it, but in that instant he was shocked out of his wits, and all other thoughts flew from his brain. "Huh?!"

He stared hard at the photo. A raven-haired girl around his own age, wearing a white bridal-veil-looking thing and a shy smile—the thought of what that must mean was a bit of a shock, but no matter how many times he tried to come up with some other explanation, there was no mistaking it: He recognized her.

Their final words to each other when he'd last seen her sprang to his mind.

We'll see each other again, won't we?
Yeah. I think we will.

He'd never imagined they'd be meeting again like *this*, of course.

A half-translucent floating spirit was drifting around near the ceiling. Kieli gazed up at it indifferently for a bit and then looked forward again.

She'd heard that long ago, when this had been an exile planet where prisoners who'd committed serious crimes on the mother planet were banished, this was where the prison camps had been, and the capital city was built on those foundations. The gray town walls surrounding it were supposedly left over from the prison camps, too. When people had eventually figured out that there were mineral resources on this planet, the prisoners were drafted into hard labor in the shafts of mines all over the planet, beginning with the district to the northwest.

This was God's city, built on the graves of those prisoners who'd been used for hard labor until they died.

All the different facilities around her formed a sort of giant sprawling complex, centered on the tallest two towers in its forest of steeples: the cathedral's belfry and the energy tower that powered the city. An ostentatious gate loomed in front of her. Evidently the pass that priest had given her was the real thing after all (which Kieli'd definitely had her doubts about), because when she showed it to the gate attendant, he completely lost his head, and once he regained his composure, he guided Kieli to the Preaching Department's tower as if she were an honored guest.

Regular pilgrims could take the central walkway from the gate and go straight to the cathedral, but getting to the Preaching Department felt like navigating a maze. Kieli was guided down winding walkways, up zigzagging steps, down dizzying spiral stairways, and through cloisters connecting towers and buildings before they finally arrived at the Preaching Department entrance. She just knew she wouldn't be able to find the way back by herself.

She ended up having to wait there for a while.

......She was about to finally meet (the man who might be) her father.

All of a sudden her hands were cold. She clenched them tightly at her sides.

She'd been offered a seat in the waiting room, but she'd refused. She waited standing still as a statue in the entryway to the tower. She could see priests dressed in black busily coming and going. Some of them darted funny looks at her as they went by, probably wondering what an obviously out-of-place girl like her was doing here. A little uncomfortable, Kieli dropped her gaze and stared at her feet.

"Hey," she murmured softly...to the one presence that ought to be right nearby. The air shifted slightly in response, and she pinpointed where it was. This man could really be inconspicuous when he chose to be. He blended into any situation, faded into the woodwork wherever he went, but with Harvey and Harvey alone there was obvious bad blood.

Kieli hated him, but she had no one else to turn to right now, and she found herself striking up a conversation with him as if it were the natural thing to do. "Do you know your dad?"

After she'd asked that, she regretted it. Joachim wouldn't know his parents any more than Harvey did.

Kieli changed the question. "...If you met your dad, what would you do?"

She knew that to him, it wasn't even a hypothetical; it was something that could never possibly happen.

"Eh...I'd kill him," he answered in a flippant whisper. Kieli found herself turning around slightly before she thought better of it. The lanky man with blue-gray eyes and a priest's outfit was looking down at her with the same thin smile as always. "I mean, it'd be creepy, right? And if he *looked* like me, that would be the pits. Think about it: there'd be another one of me!" The way he said it, he made it sound as though he couldn't stand even one of him existing already.

When Kieli turned her gaze forward again, he kept on whispering.

"Just so we're clear, I'll tell you one more time...I'm going to kill your dad, you know."

"Whatever," Kieli spat back without looking at him, and heard him give a sarcastic little closed-mouth laugh.

"I see. Well, then, have fun at your meeting."

His presence abruptly vanished. Just as she was about to turn around again, a loud voice cried, "Th-thank goodness!" and she heard clattering footsteps speeding toward her.

It was that young priest who'd come to the northwestern mining district as an envoy. Kicking up the hem of his robes in his haste, he ran to her the same way he had when they'd first met. One moment he was flapping both hands busily back and forth, wailing, "I couldn't get through to your guards, and I thought you'd r-run awa—!" and the next he broke off and nervously cast his gaze all around where Kieli stood. His face went a shade paler with surprise.

"Er, what about the people…people? with you…?" he asked, interrupting and then repeating himself weirdly (now that she thought about it, Kieli supposed someone like him really might have trouble figuring out how much like "people" to treat her companions).

When she turned around at the question to look for the slate-gray man standing behind her, he'd already melted into the stream of priests coming and going and was nowhere to be seen. She guessed maybe he was done with her now that he'd so successfully infiltrated Church headquarters. Kieli didn't feel inclined to help or hinder him, so she didn't broach the subject.

"…We got separated," she said, facing the priest again and explaining what had happened in a voice stripped of all emotion. When she gave him a bare-bones version about being attacked on the train by some monsterlike things (she didn't know if he knew what they really were, so she was deliberately vague), it turned out word apparently hadn't reached him yet. His normally pale face went even paler.

"Also," Kieli added over his earnest promises to send help right away, "the man who was with me might be hurt, so… please look for him."

She lowered her voice and narrowed her eyes in unspoken warning. *I'll never forgive you if you hurt him.* The priest visibly flinched (during that mess in the mining district Kieli herself had resisted him pretty violently, so he seemed to be afraid of her now), then turned to a lower-ranking priest nearby and gave rapid-fire orders about how to deploy the rescue team.

As he guided her inside the tower, they ended up talking about the matter at hand again—in other words, her meeting with Father Sigri. "I'm sorry, but I'm afraid you'll probably have to wait a while longer. The Father is very busy at the moment...Well, we're all in a tizzy right now," the priest explained over his shoulder as they climbed the stairs. Now that he mentioned it, she'd walked through a fair bit of headquarters on her way to the Preaching Department's tower, and it had seemed as though there was a surprising amount of uproar going on for the home base of the Church. She'd imagined someplace more solemn and dignified—or rather sedate, really.

After the broad staircase right in front of the entrance, the next set of steps was a spiral staircase along the wall. Around the time they'd climbed about three floors' worth of it and Kieli's legs were starting to get tired, the priest stopped and said, "Wait here for a few minutes, please," shepherding her toward a room next to them. Two women dressed in simple black clothes stood in front of it. Kieli assumed they were lady's maids. Leaving Kieli in their hands, the priest hurried busily off somewhere, and she was suddenly abandoned to stand all alone in front of people she didn't know. She shied back a little.

The large, somewhat overweight one glared down at her with harsh eyes that made Kieli cringe, but she glared right back just as fiercely. She'd already decided there was no way she'd let herself be intimidated in a place like this. She figured if she chickened out or licked anyone's boots here, it would mean she'd lost.

No way am I going to lose. I'm sticking this out until he comes for me.

The chubby, grumpy-looking lady-in-waiting looked her over sharply from head to toe, and Kieli found herself following her gaze and looking down at herself, too. She was still dressed in her travel clothes: the unrefined black duffle coat, beaten-up shoulder bag, dirty jeans, and dirty boots. She hadn't really bothered to untangle her hair much, either. When she glanced back at the way she'd come, she saw that she'd left clear boot prints on the glossy polished floor.

No way will I lose.

That was the plan, sure, but when they dragged her into the room, peeled off her clothes, and tossed her in the bath, it wasn't something Kieli could really protest.

In the end, it was afternoon by the time Kieli had been made presentable enough for decent company in preparation for her meeting and by the time the high-ranked man she was supposed to meet was finally free; fortunately (fortunately?), he didn't seem to have been murdered by a mysterious man in priest's clothes in the meantime.

Escorted by the same priest as before, who'd come back to get her, Kieli climbed up more stairs toward an office near the very top of the tower, almost trampling the hem of her skirt something like three times. It had been a while since she'd worn one. They'd put her in a black bolero jacket with just a thin strip of white at the neckline and a black skirt that fell below her knees with a fluffy white petticoat underneath. The whole outfit reminded her of the uniforms at her Easterbury boarding school. She was dressed up like a little lady for the first time in two and a half years.

I wonder how much I've changed since then.

She also wondered what her maybe-father would think of her when she stood before him suddenly seventeen, after they hadn't seen each other since she was a baby.

Back when she was living with her grandmother and going to the Church kids' program, whenever the other kids started going on about their moms and dads, Kieli had started playing all by herself outside the circle of conversation, pretending not to be interested. And the truth was, she hadn't even been all that interested. She'd never known her parents to begin with, so she didn't "miss" them, and since having her grandmother with her was enough for her, she didn't spend any time wishing she could meet them, either.

But ever since she'd met her mother, Setsuri, she'd thought about her father a tiny bit more, too. Still, her mental image of him had always been really difficult to put a face to. In her mind, her father figure was blank and featureless. Kieli had sometimes hoped he was someone like Jude. The Jude in Kieli's memories, though, never showed his face, either. All she had left was the strong impression that he had the same sort of vibe as Harvey. Making Harvey into her father figure was just insane, so she'd given up on that train of thought. She figured any kid with Harvey for a father would either turn delinquent, or go the opposite route and turn into someone who really had their act together.

And right now, the father figure she could imagine concretely for the first time... was someone who'd wrecked things for her mother and had tormented Harvey, Beatrix, Jude, and who knew how many others. Someone who was nothing more than Kieli's greatest enemy.

Her heart beat audibly fast in her chest. She balled her cold hands into fists.

Joachim... aren't you here?

Uneasy on her own, she found herself casting about for the gray man's presence, but she couldn't sense it anywhere.

"Please, come this way," prompted the priest. They were standing in front of the door to the room he was waiting in. Kieli yanked her thoughts back on track and lifted her eyes.

Straightening her spine and steeling herself, she looked straight ahead fiercely enough to beat back anything and everything. She was no longer the slightly nervous girl who couldn't say what she wanted to say that she'd been at fourteen. She'd come here to settle things, to protect the people she cared about, so they could all go home together.

Kieli stood in the doorway and stared straight ahead. Bookshelves crammed full of thick books covered one whole wall, and there were piles of papers sitting everywhere. It definitely looked like a civil servant's office. Rather than the lavish office of a pompous big shot that she'd been picturing, it made her think more of a novelist's study, packed with all the books it could hold; one little spark would send the whole place up in flames, no doubt about it. And behind the big writing desk at the far end of the room, she saw a person.

He seemed hard at work, talking about something with a middle-aged priest who stood next to the desk, until out of the blue he bellowed angrily, "Don't bring every tiny little approval like this to me!"

Kieli started in surprise. The middle-aged priest squeaked and shrank back, too. The forms he'd brought had just been flung back at him, and he humbly apologized as he stooped to pick up all the scattered papers before fleeing as fast as his legs would carry him past Kieli and out of the office. Jumping to the side, she watched him go.

Standing up with both hands pressed against his desk, the man, Father Sigri, noticed them there for the first time.

"Er, I've...brought her with me, sir..." the young priest who'd escorted her said hesitantly.

"A-ah, yes." Father Sigri coughed, looking somewhat embarrassed, smoothed out the worst of his disarranged hair, and sat back down in his chair before looking at Kieli again. The tightly coiled tension between them just kind of went slack for a few seconds, and they ended up staring at each other stupidly.

Kieli certainly hadn't been picturing a "touching reunion with her long-lost father" or anything; she'd just assumed and prepared herself for something more like a staring contest between mortal enemies. But there just wasn't a clear sort of "now we meet" moment. It turned into a really vague, sloppy first meeting.

The man sitting on the other side of the writing desk wasn't a nasty holier-than-thou pontiff who sat all high and mighty in his chair looking down his nose at the world, or a snake-oil-salesman sort of pontiff with a gentle manner and a fake-looking smile on his face, or even one with a greasily gleaming bald head who had gold teeth and whatnot and generally reeked of evil. No, he was a slightly disheveled, tired-looking man of medium height and slight build whose black hair was visibly starting to go gray. Beneath his thin wire glasses his eyes were lighter than Kieli's, and the solid, heavy desk didn't suit him, although the piles of books did—basically, he didn't give the impression of a stately pontiff at all, whatsoever.

He seemed bewildered by the weird beginning to their meeting, too, at a loss for words for a little while. Then he pasted a highly awkward smile on his face and said, "Well... um, thank you for coming such a long way." The sentiment was slightly out of line with the mood of the room and delivered in a tone as awkward as the smile.

Kieli stood rooted to the ground, dumbstruck. The truth was that her knees were knocking, and she felt as if she might crumple to the ground any second. Her head was swimming with confusion. He was just so—so *normal*.

I came here to hate you, maybe even kill you if I had to! So why are you putting on that dumb-looking smile and saying stuff like you're trying to get on my good side?!

All of a sudden Kieli was mad. Because the ham-handed but earnest way he tried to string words together sort of reminded her of the way Harvey had been acting lately. So she was mad, because she couldn't forgive her worst enemy for seeming like Harvey. *Don't try to act like Harvey!*

"Would you come a little closer...?"

He stood up from his chair and reached out a hand to her. Kieli took a step back in defiance. Folding her arms in front of her chest to shield herself, she said, "I still...haven't gotten the full story. You might have the wrong person—"

At her stony rejection, he gave her a blank look, one hand still stretched out toward her.

"You couldn't possibly be the wrong person. You look just like Setsuri."

"You don't..."...*have the right to say my mother's name.* She went hoarse before she could get the rest of the words out, and the sentence petered into nothing. Kieli bit her lip and looked down. *No, no, I can't lose,* she told herself, and forcibly held on to her brave attitude. "Then why did my mother...why did she have to leave here? Mom...got killed by the Church...!"

There was silence for a few moments. Father Sigri's voice lowered gloomily. "Yes, I heard the report."

The instant Kieli heard that, the mental thread she'd been somehow managing to hang on to snapped with no warning, and two thick tears trickled down her cheeks and dropped to her feet. She could sense Father Sigri, and the priest standing next to him anxiously watching the proceedings, panic. Kieli summoned up the strongest attitude of rejection that she could muster and roughly wiped the wetness from her face with her sleeve. Slowly edging farther backward until she reached the doorway, she said shrilly, "I will never, ever forgive you. I hate you. I hate this place. It's noisy, and everyone's in a hurry, and they all look tired, and they don't care one bit how anybody feels...and they shove you into a bath and make

you wear clothes you don't want to wear...!" Kieli clenched the hem of her skirt tightly in her fists. "It's a lie that I was born here. It's a lie that my mom was ever here. Because I hate this stupid place! There isn't even a God here...!"

In the astonished silence that followed Kieli suddenly flying off the handle, her hitched, teary voice echoed hollowly. She'd come here to boldly settle things, but the way she was acting right now, she might as well be a little girl throwing a tantrum. Kieli knew that. Still, now that the feelings had exploded out of her, she couldn't rein them in no matter how hard she tried.

"God isn't even real...! Harvey knows, too; he said so! But all of you go around pretending there's a God; you should be ashamed! And it's the people here's fault that Harvey's had to be on the run all this time, and gotten so beaten up, and...and I hate you all! I hate everyone here! All of you—all of you just drop dead!"

At her screaming, the big, fat lady-in-waiting from before seized her and pinned her arms.

She couldn't remember very clearly later, but she probably kept right on screeching *All of you drop dead* as she was dragged out of the room, and that was how Kieli's first meeting with her "father" ended up a mess of her own making.

This particular story of the "Eleven Saints and Five Families" era was nothing more than an oral tradition now:

Legend had it that among the Five Families whose role was to serve and aid the Eleven Saints, there was one family with what you might call mage-like powers, and its members had resolved spiritual phenomena, counseled and made prophecies for the Eleven Saints, and performed other such tasks. However, the Council of Elders harbored misgivings about how this family's influence over the faithful had steadily increased since the pioneering era, and so they suppressed its voice in state affairs. The Council of several generations ago had made a taboo of the "spiritual phenomena" themselves, until the very existence of such phenomena could not be acknowledged.

Well, it was about seventeen years ago now that Lord Sigri, who was related by blood to one of the Eleven Saints, had married a descendant of that family, Setsuri, in order to assimilate her persecuted line into his own (or perhaps Lord Sigri had intended to preserve her line by doing this), and they'd had a daughter.

Happiness didn't last long, however. One day during worship, one of the Elders fell from the tower and died, shocking everyone, and for certain reasons the blame was laid at Setsuri's door. Setsuri wasn't actually sentenced to any punishment, but the Council of Elders obliterated her from all records, and she vanished from the capital along with the baby, who wasn't even a year old yet. The connection between Setsuri's disappearance and the fact that Lord Sigri was promoted to Elder immediately afterward was...unknown, officially speaking.

It all happened right before Julius was born, and so on paper, the only baby born during that time period with the blood of one of the Eleven Saints was a boy named Julius.

"Dad, did you know this woman Setsuri?" Julius asked his father after he heard the story. His father stroked his chin, looking thoughtful.

"I can't say she ever talked very much, but I got the impression she had a core of strength. He took a formidable woman for his wife, I always thought...I have to say, it just amazes me that you know Lord Sigri's daughter. It really is a small world."

Then his father straightened his hunched shoulders and grinned at him. "Do you like her?"

"No, I—"

The way Julius blushed beet-red and fell speechless in the middle of his answer wouldn't have fooled anyone. But instead of pressing the issue like Julius feared, his father looked away with a conflicted expression and muttered, "Mmm, blood will tell, I suppose."

Puzzled, Julius thought over what that meant.

"Dad, don't tell me you had feelings for Setsuri...? B-but you had Mom!"

"Now, now, that was a long time ago," his father explained glibly, raising his hands as if in surrender when Julius angrily stepped toward him. "I couldn't save Setsuri either." After a long pause, he muttered, "I'm just as guilty as Sigri."

Apparently it was after that incident that his father and Father Sigri had drifted apart.

Father Sigri was away from his office for meetings and services and whatnot, so it was the evening of the day after Julius's conversation with his father when he finally got permission to meet with Kieli.

They'd gotten word that monsters had attacked the freight train, and Julius's father had tried to send a rescue team right away, but his men reported that by the time they arrived, a platoon of Undying Hunters had already cleaned up the scene. His father had looked highly dissatisfied with this news. So far the Undying Hunters, who were controlled directly by the Council of Elders, always stole a march on him whenever it came to incidents related to the mysterious monsters.

Julius was led by a large lady-in-waiting so grumpy that even he shrank back from her a little to a room in one corner of the top floor of the Preaching Department tower. Most likely it was a night duty room, either for Father Sigri himself or for one of the high-ranking priests under him; it looked as though it was probably trimmed with all the comforts she could require, but it was locked from the outside. Julius frowned. "She got agitated and became a bit violent, you see," the lady-in-waiting explained in a monotone.

Just one room, with a bed and a desk by the wall. The lighting was rather low, with city lights shining faint beams through the arched window. Beside the window stood a girl in black clothes with long black hair.

Looking at her profile as she glanced out the window with downcast eyes, Julius's heart jumped just a little in his chest.

"Juli," the girl said calmly when she noticed him, not sounding especially surprised as she turned to face him. Her voice was hard, as if rejecting something. And yet at the same time, her black eyes were slightly misty; she looked as if she might cry any second. Julius forced a soft smile onto his face.

"Are you okay, Kieli?"

The girl nodded wordlessly.

Instructing the lady to wait in the hallway, he entered the

room alone and closed the door. Kieli was waiting by the window. He didn't know if it was because it'd been almost six months since he'd last seen her and he'd gotten a little taller in the meantime, but when he faced her, this girl a year older than him seemed smaller than he remembered, for some reason. Still, he was sure he didn't come close to that guy's height.

"This really surprised me. For a lot of reasons."

"Me too," Kieli agreed, looking downward. "That big-shot Church Soldier really was your father, huh?" *Big-shot Church Soldier? . . . Oh, she means Dad.* Around the end of winter his father had been gone from the capital for more than a week; Julius had since been told that he'd gone at Father Sigri's request, as protection for the envoy sent to meet Kieli. From what his father said, there'd been a redheaded Undying with her, but . . .

"Where is he?" Julius asked hesitantly.

"He's coming for me later," came the answer immediately, in the most stubborn voice he'd ever heard her use.

"'Later'? Kieli, security is tight right now. He won't have an easy time getting into the capital without a pass."

Kieli just said, "He's coming for me," and shook her head. "He promised me."

She insisted so stubbornly that, without thinking, Julius grabbed her shoulder a little roughly, intent on making her see sense. "Kieli!" She flinched away and glared at him with hostility. "Oh—I-I'm sorry." He hastily withdrew his hand. Angry with himself for frightening her, he tried to somehow change the subject.

"Sorry . . . Um, tell me if there's anything you need, or if you've run short of anything, okay? I have to go to school tomorrow, but I'll come back again the day after."

Kieli only shook her head to show him she didn't want anything. Then she lowered her head and said softly, "I'm sorry..." Julius didn't know what she was apologizing for at first—not until she continued.

"I know I said you were like the prince of some noble family back then...but, you know, I wasn't jealous of you at all. I don't need the Church's God. 'God' never does anything for us. See, Juli, a little while ago I told everybody here to drop dead. And I meant it. And...that included you, too. So, I'm sorry...I can't let you be nice to me. I don't have the right."

Her words were a stab straight through his heart.

She wasn't to blame for that, though. It was just coming home to him how naive and thoughtless he was.

The truth was, when Julius had found out there was a kid his own age with the same kind of family name he had, and that it was Kieli, he'd been overjoyed. He'd thought it was *perfect*, in fact. He'd wondered before whether, if Father Sigri had had a child, they could've been friends. And then his fantasy had come true, and as if that weren't enough, it was Kieli of all people.

So the truth was, he'd come here to see her feeling kind of on top of the world. And now he felt as though someone had pushed him off a cliff. It came home to him how he'd been thinking only of himself. From Kieli's perspective, the truth about her birth had been shoved in her face out of the blue, and the only feelings she had about it so far were disorientation and rejection. Now she was shut up in this tiny room all alone, and she'd been trying her hardest to hide how lonely and scared she felt with that stony attitude. He finally realized that now. Painfully clearly.

Ugh, I was just happy for myself. I didn't have a clue how she felt coming here, what she must have prepared herself to risk entering enemy territory like this. He'd grown a lot taller than her by now, but he was still far from an adult; he couldn't think of anything to say to this isolated girl. Kieli stayed obstinately silent.

"I'll come back the day after tomorrow..." he somehow managed to force out. Then he left the room.

"Dammit," he swore after he'd made it into the hallway. *I'm no match for him.* It stung—it was really infuriating—but he couldn't be enough of a support for her. He was acutely, painfully aware that he just couldn't take *that guy's* place. Not that Julius could see what was so great about him, frankly. But even still...he was no match for him. He never would be, no matter how tall he got or how many years passed.

Where the hell is he?

From what he could tell, they'd gotten split up when the monsters attacked the miners' train. As he pondered whether he could use his father's connections to track the guy down, he directed his feet not toward home, but to the office of the person in charge of the entire Preaching Department.

He spotted Father Sigri right outside his office, evidently just coming back from some meeting or other.

At his call of "Lord Sigri," that man far, far out of Julius's league—a member of the Council of Elders, the highest organ of Church authority—turned to face him. Another priest whose name Julius didn't know trailed after the Father off to one side. An aide, by the look of him. He was the same priest who'd made the arrangements for his meeting with Kieli. For a moment Father Sigri's expression said he didn't know who Julius was, but then he gave a friendly, if tired, smile. "Ah, Julius. That's right, you came to check on her, didn't you? How was she?"

Julius ignored the question. "My father instructed me to come here," he announced in a hard voice. This was the other job his father had asked him to do. Father Sigri tilted his head somewhat warily.

Julius took a breath, firmed his resolve, and said it in a clear voice:

"Why is the Council of Elders covering up the monster incidents that have been cropping up recently?"

Instantly, all expression quietly disappeared from Father Sigri's face. The priest hovering behind him jumped up, pale-faced and obviously about to say something along the lines of *How dare this child say such a thing?!*

"I'm sorry, but I don't have the time to sit down and chat with you. I have another meeting...yes, a meeting to discuss Father Gus's funeral arrangements. I have to go."

"This is a message from my father."

Father Sigri turned on his heel to leave, keeping his composure but very obviously evading him. Julius circled around in front of him and spread both arms wide to block his path.

Staring seriously up at the Elder, who was a bit taller than he was, he called his father's lines to mind and delivered them verbatim, careful not to leave out a single word.

"None of the Council geezers were long for this world in the first place, so why are you wasting your time burying them instead of dealing with what's killing people in this city right now?" He took a deep breath. "Forget about a few senile old fools who were practically dead anyway, and do some work!"

Julius left his father's last line as a parting shot and then turned around and fled as fast as his legs could carry him while Father Sigri was still speechless with shock.

Man, that felt good.

"Wh-who does that boy think he is?!"

"He's my friend's son."

The priest raised his voice harshly. "Be that as it may, the language that he used—"

"No, it's fine. Let him be," said Father Sigri calmly enough, although his face had lost some of its color. The priest was bristling with anger at the retreating boy, but at that, he had no choice but to back down.

"Would you go check on my daughter for me? I have to go back out again right away."

With that final order, Father Sigri went into his office. The priest said to his retreating back, "Y-yes, Father. I will," bowing hurriedly and setting out for the young lady's room, thinking, *"Practically dead"... he's got a point.*

He couldn't stifle a chuckle, and although no one was watching, he quickly schooled his features. The truth was, he actually felt a strange sort of respect (just a little, of course; nothing too drastic) for the boy who'd delivered that line no one could safely say out loud in the capital and then bolted.

Really, he was supposed to be starting his job as a part-time lecturer at the seminary at the beginning of the school year that began this spring; but since he'd been made Father Sigri's envoy to his daughter, he'd just sort of become the man's unofficial aide over the course of things, and in the end he was still trailing after the Elder everywhere he went. Most of his duties involved taking care of the Elder's daughter, who'd just arrived in the city, and guarding the woman Undying currently imprisoned in the Elder's house (maybe "running errands for her" would be more accurate). He was in charge of all the Elder's personal problems, basically. Most likely serving at an Elder's side was a far better shortcut to promotion than being some part-time lecturer. Although if the Elder were to fall from power, he'd be falling right along with him ...

So far this information was need-to-know only so as not to confuse the average believer, but right now the upper echelons of the capital were in chaos. The thing was, starting with the First Elder's peaceful death last fall and continuing in the first months of this year, four (practically dead) Elders had dropped dead in rapid succession. The first two deaths had been from heart failure, and considering the Elders' ages, there hadn't been much of a stir beyond the usual fuss over who would replace them—but the third and fourth deaths had been abnormal. The third Elder had died suddenly after vomiting blood. And the fourth...a lady-in-waiting had discovered him one morning hanging from the ceiling fans in his private rooms. That Elder's death hadn't been made known yet, nor had there been a public funeral.

All sorts of rumors were circulating—some said an assassin was targeting the Elders, and some even whispered about taboos like a curse by the First Elder from beyond the grave. That was when the atmosphere in the upper levels of the city had begun to grow uneasy. Aggravating the situation even further was the Council of Elders' internal rivalry over who had the right to use the unexploded bomb brought in from Westerbury.

Before he knew it, the very echo of his own footsteps in the darkened corridor spooked him. These days they might all be doing their jobs as if nothing were wrong, but beneath that veneer of normality the rumors about the Elders' deaths and the fear hanging over them all never ended. The armed guards dispatched by the Security Forces were crawling around everywhere, even inside the Preaching Department, and the fact that the two departments didn't exactly get along just served to strain the atmosphere even further.

And add to that the spate of monster attacks in the streets... Looking back on it, he felt as though the Elders had started dying off and the monsters had started attacking right around the same time that unexploded bomb had been carried into town...Well, maybe he was overthinking things.

Compared to the job in the country he'd always complained about being so bored with, he'd been living on the scene of unbelievable storms and conspiracies ever since he picked up that woman Undying.

He couldn't say whether it was good luck or bad luck that had summoned him to the capital when all this was going on...

He couldn't say whether it was good luck or bad luck that had summoned him to the capital when all this was going on...

⟋

It was two days after the young lady had arrived here that the priest took her out and showed her around headquarters. She appeared to have calmed down some, and it didn't seem fair to keep her shut up in her room all the time. "Please let me see Beatrix. Is she okay?" she'd pressed him several times, her attitude still stiff. But he didn't have Father Sigri's permission for that yet.

"She's so okay, she's a little *too* okay," became his answer each time. It was the honest truth, after all.

At that hour, the morning worship service was being held in the cathedral (exactly as it always was, without betraying the slightest trace of the chaos in the upper levels of the capital), with the various pilgrims from distant lands in attendance. Looking down from the choir balcony a level higher up from where he usually sat, he could see that the great hall was covered from end to end with the heads of so many people dressed up in the dark hats and shawls appropriate for worship that he could imagine making some sort of game out of whacking them down. Even though this was a time of silence, with a crowd this large gathered in the cathedral there was always a hushed rustling of people. A semicircular balcony jutted out of the upper part of the tower-like pillar adorning the center of the front wall; it was from there that Father Sigri, dressed in long pure-white robes trimmed in gold, was delivering his sermon. The majestic stained glass making up one wall cast faint colored light on the Father's back.

As always, Father Sigri's sermon filled him with admiration. Most of the time the Father wasn't the kind of person you could exactly say exuded authority (no offense intended), but he *was* technically an Elder (...no offense intended), and his lectures on the holy book were very understandable and compelling even to people with no special schooling in the subject. When he stood at the lectern, Father Sigri's voice rang low and gentle throughout the room, soaking into his audience.

"What do you think?" he asked, glancing at the profile of the young lady watching the worship service with him from the shadows of the choir.

"It's a lot bigger than the chapel in Easterbury," she answered, deliberately misunderstanding him.

After some hesitation, he tried again a little more directly. "What do you think of your father's work?"

"I still don't believe he's my father," she replied in a hard voice as she stared with her striking dark eyes, almost glared, really, at the central balcony. She might not lash out anymore like she had on the first day, but she still had that same old stubborn attitude. It made the priest wrinkle his nose a little.

She seemed to lose interest halfway through the service, abruptly turning her eyes away and striding off. Since he couldn't very well leave her alone, the priest caught up with her and walked beside her. Worship was still under way, so once they left the cathedral there was no one else in sight; the corridor was wreathed in tranquillity. From behind him he began to hear the voices of the choir.

They didn't especially have anything to talk about, and he knew that even if he tried to strike up a conversation he'd only get shut down with a gruff, curt reply; so the two of them walked side by side in uncomfortable silence for a while.

To test us, the Lord gave to us
a planet of sand and barren fields
O ye children traveling the planets, plow the wilderness and
grow wheat

"...I've been meaning to ask you something."

He was casually listening to the faraway singing when the girl spoke up of her own volition for once. "Hmm? Ah yes, what is it?" he replied, faltering a little at the suddenness of it. By now he'd grown nervous of her in spite of himself. The way he saw it, she was a highly dangerous character who might attack at any time.

Without preamble, she shot a glance over his shoulder and said, "Who is that behind you?"

"What?!" he shrieked before he could stop himself, dodging to one side and turning to look back on where he'd been standing moments ago. Naturally there was no one there, but he remembered that woman Undying saying something similar to him, and a shiver went up his spine.

The girl, on the other hand, was the very picture of calm as she continued. "Has anyone close to you passed away recently?"

"N-no!" the priest cried at once. She said only, "I see," but she was still staring intently at something behind him, tilting her head a little in thought.

"Wh-what is it...?"

"I don't think you have to worry about it. You've just got somebody watching over you, that's all."

That was all she said before abruptly turning her eyes away.

"Hey, wait, it seriously worries me when you say that!" he wailed, all the blood draining from his face, but by then she'd already started walking indifferently away. "W-wait a second, please!" The priest scurried after her, darting frequent glances over his shoulder.

Please, give me a break...

It came home to him all over again that this girl was danger-ous. *This is not funny!*

Somebody watching over you—

As he followed the raven-haired girl's rapidly retreating back, turning around every few paces to look behind him, something clicked in his memory.

The nice old folks in that hick town who'd brought by food for him all the time and treated him like their own sons or grandsons when he moved to its tiny old Church outpost to live by himself. In the beginning he'd had a hard time getting used to his job, and he couldn't adjust to the country life at all, but they'd generously accepted him into the fold. Over the five years he'd worked there, he'd sat by the peaceful deathbeds of a few of those old folks, too.

I've lived long enough. I've got no complaints. I'm glad you're here at the end to see me off.

I'll be watching over you, you hear? Hang in there...

All his seniors in life who had passed peacefully into the next world.

He'd been bored out of his mind. All he could think about was escaping. And yet, he had to admit it had been a simple life full of peace and quiet. His dream of running away had come true, with the result that here he was on the outer fringes of elite capital society, a tangled jungle of conflicting interests.

Why had he wanted so badly to get out of there back then, exactly? Had he really wanted *this*? Maybe he'd only been longing for the grass on the other side of the fence.

Was he lucky or unlucky right now?

"How was she today?" Father Sigri asked him as usual when he finally made it back to his desk that night after yet another round of annoying meetings. He *could* just go see how she was for himself, but ever since his daughter had rejected him so harshly on that very first day, the man hadn't tried to meet with her again. Come to think of it, the priest's own long-dead father had been ham-handed dealing with children, too, he remembered.

"She's a formidable young lady," he confessed honestly, thinking of that afternoon.

"She takes after her mother," the Father said with a wry, conflicted-sounding laugh.

"Um…would it be all right if I asked why your wife was banished from the capital, Father?"

Father Sigri looked up from his desk. Realizing he must have been indiscreet, the priest said, a bit panicked, "Forgive me, Father!" *This is something the Council of Elders erased from its records! If I ask about it, I might be obliterated, too!* He tried to take back the question. "If it's something I shouldn't have asked…"

"No, it doesn't matter now. If you want to know, I'll tell you."

The Father let his eyes lightly roam the empty air as if recalling something, and then, in that same penetrating low and gentle voice with which he gave his sermons, he began to speak.

⁂

That girl's a little creepy, you know.

Sometimes she'll reach her hand out when there's nobody there to reach for and just burst out laughing. I tell, you it scares me…

She heard a group of women whispering. The whole conversation had a bad vibe about it: the vibe of people trying to exclude anyone different, like when they traded mean gossip about a neighbor. It reminded her of the people in her apartment building when she lived with her grandmother—*I hear that old woman on the third floor took her "granddaughter" in off the streets*—and it filled her with unconditioned revulsion.

The whisperers now were servants dressed in black and carrying piles of balled-up sheets and silver tea trays and such, apparently on the job.

Suddenly their chatter stopped. When they all turned around at once, a woman was standing there behind them, holding a baby. A woman with her long black hair tied back in a pony-tail, wearing even simpler black clothes than the servants. She subdued the gaily gossiping crowd with a mild-mannered gaze that still managed to be strong and commanding.

Is that ... me?

"Lady Setsuri," said one of the women, and Kieli quickly realized that no, it was her mother. *Which means that baby fast asleep in her arms all wrapped up in the baby blanket is me.*

As the servants maintained an uncomfortable silence, Set-suri kept right on walking, looking undaunted. When she passed through the center of their group, the sleeping baby suddenly started fussing. Inky black eyes very like her moth-er's flickered open. She stared off into space for a while, as if she were following something floating through the air with her eyes and then giggled happily.

The images blurred away into nothing, revealing a painting hanging on the wall where they had been. It depicted in pains-taking detail ten or so people praying over the bread on their table. Kieli recognized it from her textbooks back at the boarding school as a religious painting that illustrated a scene from the holy book. In the dimness of the low-lit room, the people's eyes were dark and clouded, and their white skin stood out in sharp relief.

That was ...

She was currently sitting on the edge of the bed in the tower room she'd been assigned for her stay, gazing at a painting on the wall. The sound of silence hung in the air of the empty room.

One of the people in the painting seemed to laugh all of a sudden.

Tee-hee-hee…

Kieli could hear laughter coming from inside the painting. Just as she was leaning forward to give it a harder look, a sort of white shadow leapt out of it, and she quickly shrank back when it seemed about to hit her.

This time the laughter came from off to Kieli's side.

When she shifted her gaze toward it, her head still lowered defensively, she saw a girl standing in the corner of the room. A raven-haired girl in filmy white robes that looked almost like underwear. She looked sort of like Kieli. "Um…" Kieli called to her, but before she could say anything, the girl whirled around and vanished into the darkness.

Tee-hee-hee…

Laughter again, from a different direction.

When Kieli looked for the source of the voice, that same girl was standing in front of the door to her room this time. Giggling in a breathy whisper, she slid away through the door. The hem of her white slip fluttered like wings as it vanished through the crack between the door and the jamb.

Kieli climbed barefoot out of the bed. She didn't know if the lady-in-waiting had forgotten to lock the door or what, but when she tried the knob, the door opened with a creak. She

tentatively craned her head out into the hallway. This late at night, there was nobody in sight there. A dull, murky light shone from the electric lamps placed at wide intervals.

With a soft tap of her toes, Kieli left the room with the same bare feet and white slip as the other girl had.

Tee-hee!

She turned in the direction of the voice. She saw the hem of a slip fluttering down the hallway for just an instant before it melted away into the gloom. Kieli pointed her feet in that direction as if drawn by a magnet. Strangely, she had no hesitation or fear. For some reason she felt as though she'd known this bizarre girl for a long time.

The inside of the tower was like a maze, but whenever she seemed about to get lost, the girl's voice beckoned her. Kieli padded obediently down the cold hallway floor as she was beckoned. After several winding corridors and staircases, she came out into a wide, straight hallway with a vaulted ceiling. Engraved pillars lined the walls on both sides, with religious paintings between each one that were much larger in size than the picture in her room.

That was where Kieli came to a stop.

That girl from before was standing on the other side of the hallway; it was just like looking into a mirror. Her white slip stood out in the gloom.

"Who are you?" Her own voice echoed softly against the ceiling.

"You forgot? You always used to smile whenever you saw me." The girl pouted her lip, miffed. Then she giggled again and spread her arms wide, reaching both hands out to Kieli.

The hem of her slip fluttered high up in front of her, and then she said, "Welcome home, old friend…"

Foosh—

Though they were indoors, out of nowhere a strong wind hit Kieli straight on, and she turned her face away and squeezed her eyes tightly shut.

Psst psst psst psst…

She began to hear people whispering to each other. The next time she opened her eyes, the pictures lining both walls all began spinning at once like rewound reels of time, playing scenes from the past. Too many images flowed into Kieli's mind for her to sort through them all, giving her vertigo.

The scene in all of them was the cathedral she'd been shown today. The whole throng of people inside talked uneasily among themselves. All eyes were riveted on a spot directly below the balcony that jutted out into the main hall, where a sea of blood was forming around someone on the ground wearing the long white ceremonial robes of a clergyman. Kieli thought he was an old man, but his face was too horribly crushed to look at, let alone tell anything from. His pure-white robes were dyed crimson before her eyes, and the sea of blood oozed steadily outward like a living creature. The crowd circling him drew back fearfully.

What happened; why did he fall all of a sudden like that…?
Did he slip?

No, I saw it! I saw someone push him!

Kieli could hear their unsettled whispers. The expressions of all the people in their buzz of conversation showed from different angles in each of the paintings lining the wall. The priests had begun working to clear the bustling congregation from the room. Kieli even saw Father Sigri and Julius's father in one of the paintings, guiding people outside. They were both a lot younger than they were now. She could make out Setsuri standing next to Father Sigri, holding a baby.

Soon after the people started to follow the priests away, an enormous shadow fell over the electric lights illuminating the great hall.

Heh-heh-heh-heh-heh-heh! Kyahahahahahaha! Shrill, crazed laughter echoed over the heads of the people. The torches adorning the walls crackled and burst, and everyone began running around in terror.

Gya-ha!

A lone innocent giggle rang out, out of place in the midst of the confusion. The baby in Setsuri's arms alone seemed happy, squealing with laughter and waving her tiny hands toward a shadow where there was nothing to be seen.

"That child did it! She's demon spawn!" someone yelled, pointing at the baby. The hysterical shouts wove their way through the crowd, spreading like wildfire among people who were already at the height of fear. They fell into a frenzy and mobbed Setsuri, surrounding her and jostling as they tried to snatch the baby she protected.

Mom! Stop it. My mom—somebody help my mom! Kieli shouted with all her breath at the scene flowing into her mind, reaching out her hands. But naturally, neither her hands nor her voice could reach it. It only glided along the surface of her consciousness and then away. The baby—the baby *Kieli*, who'd been laughing up until then, burst into ear-splitting wails. The shrill, grating cries only spurred on the people's panic.

As she cradled her baby protectively to her chest, Setsuri scanned the crowd, looking for someone. Finding that someone, she extended a pleading hand for help. Kieli mentally followed the line of her mother's gaze.

Standing there a little apart from the confusion was Father Sigri. He seemed rooted to the spot, just looking on blankly as the agitated crowd elbowed him violently this way and that. He took in the frail, outstretched hand of his wife, who stood holding his daughter—and Father Sigri bit his lip and abruptly looked away.

The last thing Kieli saw before the images of the confusion went dark was Setsuri's sad black eyes.

After a period of blankness, she began to hear subdued murmurs from inside the paintings again. "Who will fill the late Eleventh Elder's seat?" "Lord Sigri was the prime candidate, wasn't he?" "But there are rumors that his daughter is a demon child..." Against the backdrop of the people's murmuring, the image of a lavish room with a heavy round table in the center formed itself within the painting. Old men sat around the table in long, adorned black robes.

Next to the lowest seat at the table, where the old men all turned their harsh looks, stood a man.

"Well, Lord Sigri?" asked the old man in the highest-ranking seat.

"Would you like to add your name to the list of men who have sat in that seat at this round table?" asked another old man.

"Are you prepared to forsake your wife and daughter?" asked another.

The ten men's twenty eyes all focused on the standing man. There was silence for a little while.

And then the man, staring straight ahead, said, "Yes."

All the religious paintings on the wall were back to regular, unmoving pictures. The girl who'd appeared from out of the painting in Kieli's room was gone, too. A cold wind blew in from the far end of the painting-lined corridor where she'd been standing just moments ago.

Kieli made her way toward that end with quiet footfalls like cold waves lapping at a shore.

The moment she stepped out of the hallway, a violent gust of wind crashed into her. Before her stretched a colonnade completely open to the elements, connecting this tower to the next one. In the gaps between the fat, evenly spaced columns she could see the towering, inky shadows of the mountains. Cold mountain wind riffled her thin slip. Her exposed skin was freezing in no time. Kieli cringed, folding her arms over her chest for warmth.

Someone was walking up the cloister toward her. Someone about medium height and skinny, wearing long, black robes that melted into the darkness around him and carrying books and papers under one arm. The long, thin edges of his glasses caught the faint outdoor light and gleamed silver, telling her who he was. Perhaps her white slip stood out in all the darkness; he noticed Kieli right away, too, and halted, seeming surprised.

Kieli spun around 180 degrees and started to flee, but a voice called after her, "W-wait!" and she slackened her pace automatically. Sigri caught up to her and grabbed her arm from behind. Momentum sent her stumbling forward, and they both ended up falling. Papers scattered over the floor, rustling. "I-I'm sorry. Are you hurt?" Apologizing clumsily, he reached down to help her up, but Kieli slapped his hand away. They both sat there for a little while at the edge of the colonnade, wordlessly catching their breaths.

Turning her face away from the man in front of her to glare at him out of the corner of her eye, Kieli said coldly, "You're still working so late?"

At her question, Sigri looked down for a moment at the papers and books littering the floor.

"Yes…there are…a lot of problems happening right now, so things are busy…"

He wore a tentative smile on his haggard, tired-looking face as he answered. Kieli lowered her eyes and tightened her fists in her lap.

"Did you want to be an Elder that badly? Badly enough to throw away Mom and me?"

Her murmur trembled a little. She could tell that Sigri was speechless. Kieli squeezed her fists even harder, tightly enough to cut off the blood to her fingertips.

After a long pause, a short, grief-choked answer came.

"I'm sorry…"

At the sight of one of the top men in the Church meekly bowing his head without a trace of dignity, Kieli felt bitterly disappointed. Not in what he looked like making his pathetic apologies. In what he *didn't*, more likely. "Stop it, please. Apologizing to me won't do anything. If you're going to apologize, apologize to Mom. Mom was…Mom was—a strong person—but…!"

Kieli remembered the images she'd seen just a little while ago. Her mother's despairing face when her father deserted them.

"…But I'm sure she wanted you to help her that day!"

She couldn't bear to let *this* man see her cry, so she lowered her head and held back the tears. One of them escaped anyway, falling with a tiny splat onto a clenched fist. Sigri covered it with his own big, thin hand. "Let me go!"

"I'm sorry…!" Kieli tried to shake him off, but he wouldn't let go. He lowered his head until his brow rubbed against the back of her captured hand. "I'm sorry, I'm so truly sorry…"

"Apologizing to me won't bring back Mom. I don't accept you being my father."

Kieli forcibly snatched her hand out of Sigri's where he bent over it in humble contrition, apologizing over and over. She whirled around and half-ran, half-stumbled back the way she'd come, leaving Sigri on the floor where he sat.

She was so disappointed. This was just unbelievable.

A top Church official was supposed to be more stuck-up, more high and mighty, more like the cocky bad guy behind the snake-oil salesman who trumpeted the teachings of some nonexistent God to mislead the public. He was supposed to be the great wall of evil blocking her path. It wasn't okay for him not to be. He'd killed Jude, he'd killed her mother, he'd hurt Harvey so badly, and he'd captured Beatrix—and it wasn't okay for the ringleader behind all kinds of unforgivable things, Kieli's most hated enemy, to be just an exhausted, normal man like that. The people Kieli loved had been tormented all this time because of a stupid little enemy like this? No, she refused to accept it. *This* wasn't enough to get her to forgive him. He didn't get to just make an easy apology. *If an easy apology like this settled things, I wouldn't even know what I came here to fight!*

Kieli ran barefoot back down the hallway. By the time she made it back to her room, she was panting hard.

She shut the door and dived straight into the bed.

Hurry up and come get me, Harvey...! she wailed at him silently. *I thought I'd reached the end of my rope. I don't want to be in this stupid place. Let's just rescue Beatrix and go home. Let's go home, right away. Can't we all go back to Easterbury and live a happy life there without ever having anything to do with these people again?*

"Harvey...Corporal..."

Her face still buried in the pillow, Kieli's murmur and her muffled sobs were swallowed up by the silence of the room.

Even as she wished for that future in her heart, she knew no amount of wishing was likely to make it come. Harvey'd said they should live in the house at the transfer station, but he definitely wasn't really picturing a future like that. Before she knew it was happening, the happy time two and a half years ago when she was fourteen, when she'd just met them and felt so sure she'd found her place to belong, had drifted far away from her. She could never get it back now.

"Yo. Whatcha crying about?" asked a voice above her suddenly. When she lifted her face from where she'd buried it in her pillow, a pair of dark blue-gray eyes, hardly distinguishable from the dimness of the room, were looking at her. *When did he . . . I guess he must have come into the room while I was out there.* A tall, lean man in priest's garb was squatting neatly with his hands around his knees by the decorative molding at the head of her bed.

Kieli shot up from the mattress and jumped to the far side of the bed. She wiped her eyes and glared at him, clutching her pillow in front of her like a shield.

Three days had gone by since he'd disappeared on her first day here.

"Where have you been?" she asked. And then, a beat later, "I thought you were going to kill him?"

Her words sank nastily into the murky dimness of the room.

"Hmm, true . . . I figured I'd be nice and wait till you finished your touching reunion with Daddy before I tore him apart, but your meeting pretty much bombed . . ." the man answered with a thin smile. Half of that might be true, but Kieli guessed that it was at least half a lie. In what little light there was, she could make out that the skin of one cheek was green and mushy. She bet he'd been crashed out somewhere, unable to move again.

"So, whatcha crying about?" he inquired again insincerely, and grinned. He must know why already, too, the jerk. She sniffed, embarrassed. Then she scowled at the floor and quietly began to answer him. Kieli didn't understand herself what made her speak so openly to this jerk, but a part of her actually felt as though he was exactly the one she could confess something like this to. "...I was so sure there was a big enemy here, and that if I beat him, all my problems would be solved. But there isn't one..." *Just a normal, tired man who regrets what he did.* "It's not fair! What am I supposed to hate now...?"

As she spoke, she realized that she was the same as that old engineer on the miners' train, that there was a darkness deep inside her heart, and it crushed her. She was like that crotchety old man who could only cope with the pain of losing someone he loved by hating someone else and taking it out on them.

Kieli must be the type who needed to have an enemy, too. The people special to her kept being lost one after another, and she couldn't rest until she'd made that someone else's fault. Even though she was sure Harvey didn't see it that way. Harvey was someone who could forgive those who trespassed against his own interests without any trouble. She was so small-minded compared to him.

With no warning, someone was messily ruffling the hair on her lowered head. She hadn't noticed him moving, but all of a sudden Joachim was crouching right in front of her.

"There, there, no need to cry," he said, as if he were soothing a baby. Kieli stiffened uncomfortably, but she didn't resist. Though she didn't know why, his voice made her want to cling to it like a lifeline. It sounded calm and kind, but at the same time it had a sort of darkness to it like the sky at night. Her ears soaked it up.

"You and I are birds of a feather. So you know what? I'll give you a hand with this. I'll kill your enemy for you."

When his voice disappeared, all sense of his presence had bled away into the darkness again, too.

Hugging her pillow with her head bowed, Kieli stayed unmoving for a while. She felt sort of delirious, as if she had a fever. Nebulous half-formed thoughts swirled around and around in her head.

I'll give you a hand with this. I'll kill your enemy for you.

And she hadn't told him not to. She'd kind of felt that if someone would do that for her, she really wouldn't mind.

An image of Harvey's face flitted through the back of her head. Those coppery eyes always looked about to cry whenever Kieli made a mistake. Right now, one of them was dark brown instead. . . . *It's no good.*

Clutching her pillow tightly, she thought with conviction, *It's wrong, I just know it. I'm about to make another mistake.*

"Joachim . . . !"

Kieli finally came back to her senses and looked up. She was the only presence left now in this room ruled by darkness. After stiffening for just a split second, Kieli slipped out of bed. Before she shot out of the room in her bare feet, she tossed the pillow she was still hugging back onto the mattress.

His soul is too starved, it's not tasty...
Would it at least make a decent snack, though...?
Maybe we'll eat him...

Whispering raspingly to each other, the shadowy people-shapes slithered out of a corner of the room on their bellies. They crawled along the floor with eerily long, crookedly bony hands and feet toward the man standing in front of the writing desk. They stopped short midway there, though.

You again... Are you getting in our way?
You don't have a soul. We can't eat you. You're only in the way...

When Joachim spared them a glance, they withdrew to the corner of the room again, leaving accusing whispers behind them as they melted away into the darkness.

The man in long robes who'd just set his pile of documents on the desk noticed someone else in the room with him and moved to turn around. "Don't turn." Joachim cut him off by seizing one of his arms from behind and twisting it up, thrusting the folding knife against his throat. The man stopped moving with a tiny moan.

In a reedy voice, he asked, "Who *are* you?"

"The grim reaper," Joachim answered coolly.

The man's shoulder joint creaked audibly. Contorting his

body, he managed to bear the strain, though it was difficult, and when he spoke, his voice sounded pained. Still, he resolutely asked again, "You're the assassin, then...?"

"Aw, you're giving me too much credit. But hey, if you people want to make the criminal a human you can see with the naked eye, I don't mind taking the credit."

"Are you going to kill me?"

"Yep. Do you want to beg for your life?"

It was almost an innocent question, really. Still, even as he sweated greasily from the pain in his shoulder, the priest neither pleaded nor fought back. Joachim didn't know if the guy was acting tough or what, but the unexpectedly calm response took the wind out of his sails a little. That greasy old geezer he'd killed last time (well, no, he'd wormed his way into the man's good graces while intending to kill him, but the ghosts had beaten him to the punch and cursed him to death first) had begged plaintively for his life even after he kicked the bucket. Joachim had a hard time understanding why this man wasn't getting scared and begging for his life like that.

"Come on, beg for your life," he whispered, drawing his face in close to the neck he pressed his knife against. But the man only gazed at the floor with a resigned, philosophical expression on his face. He had this vibe that said he'd taken it upon himself to carry a load of fruitless, pointless guilt around with him everywhere when nobody'd ever asked him to—a vibe a lot like *that bastard's*, which made Joachim abruptly pissed off as hell.

Snik.

An incongruous, dry, inane sound. He'd given the priest's

twisted arm another hard twist and dislocated the shoulder joint.

A thin cry escaped the man's mouth. However, he still didn't resist.

Joachim found himself being questioned again instead. "...What are you trying to accomplish? What are you doing these things for?"

"What am I doing them for?" Considering who was the killer and who was the victim here, Joachim didn't see why he was the one being interrogated—and anyway, at the moment he wasn't actually the serial Elder killer; it was the evil ghosts who were cursing them all to death...But the question intrigued him a little. He experimentally tried answering from an assassin's perspective. "Because I want to kill people. They piss me off, so I'm gonna tear them all apart."

"Mm-hmm...And? What are you going to do after that?"

Joachim was so thrown off by the unexpected question that he broke character. "What do you mean, 'after that'?"

A line of blood welled up from the man's neck where the blade touched him. *Beg for your life. Plead pathetically like all the other old geezers*, he thought, pressing down on the knife, but the man's voice was quiet even as his face twisted against the agony in his dislocated shoulder. Joachim even saw him give a self-mocking smile.

"I had something I desired, too, once. I've sacrificed all kinds of things to get it. But once I reached a position where I *could* actually get it, all of a sudden I couldn't figure out what it was I'd wanted anymore. I realized all I'd been doing was grasping after a stupid ideal that didn't exist...And by that time, I'd already sacrificed something that couldn't ever be gotten back.

"I was a fool...I was a fool for hoping I could go back and atone for my sins after all this time, for ever hoping for even one minute that I could get her back..."

Joachim had left the room and pushed the door closed behind him when he heard the slap of bare feet running toward him. The girl who appeared from the end of the hallway caught sight of him and came to a stop.

She caught her breath and swallowed once before asking, "Did...did you kill him?" Her face was white as a sheet. Joachim shrugged one shoulder and gestured to the door behind him with his eyes.

"His shoulder's dislocated, so why don't you go take care of him?"

The girl turned her gaze to the door. She took a step, then changed her mind and stopped. After hanging her head, looking undecided for a bit, she turned back the way she'd come. "I-I'll go get someone to come...!" Joachim merely spared her a glance before he started walking in the opposite direction.

"Joachim—" she called tentatively. He turned a little. She'd stopped, too, and turned toward him. She opened her mouth to speak, but then she got a conflicted look on her face, as if she couldn't decide what she wanted to say in the end. Joachim clicked his tongue deliberately loud enough to hear.

"You're nothing like me after all."

Then he abruptly broke eye contact and resumed walking. She called his name one more time, but he didn't turn around again.

What's your deal? he thought. *You got worried and came running! I was going to do it for you because it was what* you *wanted, and you really didn't want me to after all!* He felt pissed off. At everything around him. At that girl, and that man who gave pompous, complicated speeches instead of begging for his life, and *that idiot* who always managed to hover like a shadow at the edges of Joachim's consciousness even when he wasn't around.

But you didn't kill him, either . . .
Why didn't you kill him . . . ?

The ghosts were whispering mockingly from a corner of the hallway. When he shot them a glare out of the corner of his eye, they slipped away into the wall, their mockery still hanging in the air. His own footsteps echoed in the shadows as he walked alone down the deserted hallway. The heavy *plop, plop* of the sticky substance dripping from the fingertips of his dangling left hand accompanied them. A little while later he started to hear the bustle of a crowd forming behind him.

What are you trying to accomplish?

He hated everything, so he'd figured if he destroyed everything, the world would become something that pleased him.

And? After that?

What do you mean, "after that"?

He experimentally stretched his left hand out in front of him. Hyperactive cells welled up from between his fingers and *plop, plop*ped down to the floor in rotting clumps. His fingernails had already lost their original shape. He glimpsed exposed bone at his knuckles.

What I wanted…

He watched the mushy cells dribble from his fingertips for a while, with no expression on his face.

INTERLUDE: THE WORLD GOES ON A LITTLE
FURTHER, A LITTLE FURTHER

It was quite late at night by the time she got the phone call from her husband. He was calling to tell her they'd be staying over at the station that night and he couldn't get home—and to remind her to make double-sure she locked up the whole house. She checked the rooms on the second floor and their balconies, then went to look at each of the windows in the first-floor hallway facing the front garden. The view of uptown Gate Town outside looked no different than any other night; it was wrapped in such still silence that somehow it seemed only natural to quiet her own breathing.

In the last month or so, there had been a rash of attacks on citizens over in the downtown slums by mysterious monsters. There'd been that fuss last fall about the dead monster falling from one of the waterway exits, and for a while that had been all anybody in town talked about, but things had just quieted down at last—and then, before they'd had the chance to draw a proper breath, *this*.

Her husband worked at Gate Town's Security Forces outpost, and recent events had him on duty around the clock more often than usual. She herself wasn't working now, but until about two years ago she'd been nursemaid to the son of a certain noble house at Church headquarters in the capital.

I hope young master Julius is all right...

She'd heard that several similar incidents had happened in the capital recently, too. Julius had just gone back to the capital the other day to prepare for the new semester after paying her a much-anticipated visit during his between-semester break. He'd answer her when she asked him how school was going and such, but it was rare now for him to guilelessly talk to her about whatever crossed his mind as he once had. On the one hand, she was proud of how he'd grown, but on the other hand, she missed what they'd once had, too. She and her husband had no children. To her, Julius was like her very own son.

"Hmm...?"

On the verge of locking the only open window, she stopped and peered into the front garden in the dim glow of their porch light. The garden gate was ajar. She thought she'd closed it, but perhaps a strong gust of wind had blown it open?

A not-insubstantial thrill of fear shivered down her spine.

E-everything's fine, she told herself. She locked the window and double-checked it and was just about to walk away when she thought she saw a shadow moving in one corner of the garden. "Wh-what was that...?" She tried to persuade herself it was only her imagination, even though she knew better, but that was when something rustled outside the window.

Her heart jumped with fright. She managed to swallow back a scream, but her legs were rooted to the spot and she couldn't get them to move. Clasping both hands in front of her chest, she stared outside.

D-darling, what should I do...?!

But the husband she silently cried to for help wouldn't be coming home tonight. Her limbs trembled. The lady scolded her uncooperative knees and determinedly began to shuffle away from the wall, when—

Bam!

Something smacked against the windowpane.

This time she *did* let out a shriek, pitched much higher than her normal speaking voice, and in her rush to scramble backward, her foot slipped and she fell to the floor. Once down, fear robbed her limbs of their strength, and she couldn't get back up. The thing plastered to the window slid down the glass and out of sight. What stayed behind on the pane were the blood-red human fingerprints.

A hand... a person's hand?!

She came back to her senses with a jolt. Though she still felt limp, she immediately crawled over to the window again, gripped the frame with both hands, and pulled herself up to her knees. When she took a careful peek outside, someone was lying collapsed next to the wall underneath the window. There was a red streak along the wall where his fingers had trailed down from the glass.

That lanky one-armed frame illuminated by the faint porch light was one the lady remembered very well. Leaning on the wall for support, she somehow managed to haul her shaking body upright and walk over to the front door. She opened it and dashed out into the garden, running toward the man slumped below her window. Still sprawled out, he was trying to gather up small bits of something or other that were scattered on the ground around him with his one tattered, blood-covered arm.

"Oh, dear!" the lady gasped. For a few moments she just stood there petrified. Noticing her, he lifted his coppery head groggily. Yes, he was definitely the young man she remembered, almost unchanged. Now that she got a look at him, it was more than just his arm that was hurt; his whole body was horribly battered.

After the young man had gazed up at her face for a while

with mismatched eyes that couldn't quite seem to converge on one point, he finally seemed to bring her into some sort of focus, and he opened his mouth uncertainly.

"Oh—sorry, I just sort of ended up here...and I couldn't think of anyplace else to go...I'll leave right away, so—if you could maybe—lend me some tools..."

His voice was scratchy and scarcely audible, and he was still trying to talk. The lady crouched in front of him and took his bloody upside-down body into her arms. "For now just come inside—please come inside—I need to bandage you—"

"I'm fine—I'm—fi—" The young man seemed half-unconscious; he was talking in choppy, feverish-sounding bursts, both speaking and acting a bit off. Neither his gaze nor his gestures were quite steady.

"Are there—still any parts on the ground? Can you look—for them for me...? My eyes—aren't too good—right now..."

He patted the ground with his lacerated hand. Come to think of it, she'd been wondering what he'd been trying to pick up all this time; now she saw what looked like parts of a machine littering her front yard. Beneath the fallen man's body, he was lovingly sheltering an old radio. And with his gaze wandering aimlessly, he was feeling around for its scattered parts by hand. "Corporal—wait a sec—we'll pick them up—sorry..." The poor thing must be very confused. He kept mumbling things that didn't really make sense to her.

"Oh, dear Lord..." the lady wailed tearfully, lifting her eyes to Heaven for a moment. Then she hurried to help him.

She found herself silently complaining to God above before she could help herself. *Why is he in such terrible condition every time we meet? Could this good-hearted young man really have committed so great a sin? Why do you give him such painful trials…?*

❧

He'd thought the world was ending. When he couldn't hear the radio anymore and even his field of vision was getting sketchy, he felt on the verge of losing track of the sound and light that connected him to the world.

His visual field in the left eye he'd gotten from Mane had shrunk to almost nothing, putting pressure on the field of his right eye, too, until everything looked dark. Harvey'd faced death dozens—make that hundreds—of times before, but the next time something happened, he really might not be able to come back again. When that thought struck him, he realized he was terrified beyond anything he'd ever felt before.

And now he was sitting in the entryway of the lady's mansion. Using the tools he'd borrowed, Harvey clumsily tinkered with the radio one-handed, based on what he'd picked up from watching other people, until he'd more or less gotten it back together. When he was done, he apprehensively turned it on.

He heard a feeble snap of static. He addressed it almost prayerfully. "Cor…poral…?"

Ksh, kshht…bzzz…crrr…!

"Corporal…?"

Kshht, bzzz…

The radio forced an uneven stream of noise out of its warped speaker, as though it was trying to say something.

"......bie...kay..." *It's okay. I'm still here.*

That's what it sounded like.

Harvey felt something warm rising in his throat, and he bit his lip and pressed his forehead to the speaker.

"That's special to you, isn't it?" he heard a voice say. When he raised his face to look, the lady was standing in front of him with a mild smile. He smoothed out the expression on his face, embarrassed, and nodded.

Harvey remembered slipping past the Undying Hunters before they noticed him and veering away from the path of the train tracks, but after that point he had only scraps of memories. He'd found himself in Gate Town without any real idea how he'd gotten there or when he'd even decided to come. Half-madly, he'd retraced his memories from all those months ago to get to this house. Even though he'd intended never to indebt himself to this lady again, he just couldn't think of anything else to do.

She sank to her knees in her pinafore and sat next to him. Harvey flinched a little when he saw that she'd brought disinfectant and wet towels and things with her. "It's okay—I think you know this, but—I'm..."...*an Undying.*

The lady shook her head before he finished. "You're going to get blood all over my floor like this. Injured people should quietly do as they're told, I'll have you know."

When she put it that way, he couldn't protest anymore, and so he ended up quietly letting himself be treated. It was just the same as when he'd been in her care in lockup half a year ago, and it was thoroughly embarrassing. He'd already healed himself a good bit on his own power, but his left arm was still badly scratched up, and the disinfectant stung. It was a different kind of pain from being wounded in the first place; one he wasn't used to. For a second he thought he might make a sound. For whatever reason, though, he didn't shut out the hurt.

Tending to his wounds in a businesslike way (Harvey wondered if she was so practiced at it because Julius had been a real little devil as a kid—he could picture that), the lady said mildly, "I'm glad to see you again. You've been in my thoughts. Is the young lady well?"

"I think so…" he mumbled vaguely, nodding. He was worried like crazy about Kieli, but there was no way for him to find out how she was doing right now. "Sorry for…causing you trouble a-gain…" He bobbed his head at her on the last syllable. "Um." Harvey couldn't think of a good way to ask this. "Why did you help…" The words stuck in his throat, and he ended up sounding kind of pathetic. Frankly, he felt pretty damn pathetic right now, barging into someone's house uninvited because he didn't have anywhere else to go, and now indebting himself further by getting taken care of like this.

"Because I think you're not a bad person."

"…That's all?"

"Do I need another reason?" The lady stilled her hands for a moment and tilted her head. Then she smiled at him, looking a little amused.

"You're a normal human being, aren't you? If I see someone who's injured and in trouble, I help them. Isn't that only normal?"

Harvey hung his head, unable to answer. He couldn't exactly

place why, but somehow it made sense to him now that this was the woman who'd raised Julius. *So normal human beings ... are allowed to let other people help them?*

Oh. Huh.

He'd never thought about that before.

"...... While I'm causing you trouble anyway, I have a favor to ask. Would you be able to contact Julius?"

He found himself broaching the favor as if it was totally natural. He'd hardly ever asked someone else to help him for free before. He knew full well he was taking advantage of her kindness to ask too much.

But the thing was, it was getting difficult to do all this on his own power.

Maybe it would be okay for him to turn to someone else.

Fzzsh ... bzzz ... crrrrrr ...

"...*bie*..."

A barely audible voice seeped from the speaker on a wave of static.

"Yeah ... Yeah, Corporal. I hear you."

Harvey pressed his forehead against the speaker and spoke slowly. "What, you were saying you weren't gonna kick the bucket yet, right?" *Kshht.* The radio answered him with slightly stronger static, as if to say *You better believe it.* That normal, everyday answer had him finally smiling a little, too. The horribly bent speaker only put out noise that barely formed meaning anymore, but Harvey could still sense for sure that their reliable guardian was there.

"It's okay. I get it. I get exactly what you're saying."

"...m...kay..."

"Yeah, I'm okay too. I still have to go meet up with Kieli, after all."

The lady went to bed first, and midnight found Harvey on his knees in front of the window facing the second-floor balcony, watching Gate Town's nighttime skyline. To his extremely bad vision, the city lights were fuzzy like fireflies; he could only just barely make out the milky-white town wall looming far beyond them. On top of his failing eyesight, the fact that he was missing a big chunk of his memories of the journey here also worried him. There was an ever-present dull pain deep behind his left eye, slowly eating its way into his brain.

The nerves will probably be infested little by little no matter what, so I think you'll end up blind eventually.

He did remember Mane saying that, but it made him somewhat anxious that things were going bad so much faster than he'd expected.

You're getting off easy if you only lose the eye, though...

"......"

Harvey squinted at the indistinct town wall in his vision.

On the other side of that wall lay his destination, the capital. The work he had to take care of was waiting there, and so was Kieli.

Harvey heard a dog barking off somewhere in the distance. The lady had told him that sightings of those failed Undyings were happening unusually often lately; he wondered if there was more outflow from the lab than before. According to her, there was some sort of disturbance going on inside the capital, too.

All kinds of things that had been slowly growing closer were rapidly picking up speed now, starting to come together...

Harvey let the grim look on his face soften and relaxed his shoulders.

He dropped his gaze to the radio he'd placed on his knees and pressed his forehead lightly against the speaker again. When he closed his eyes, even though he couldn't hear its voice, he could pick up the faint sound of its usual static. He drew a relieved breath. His vision might be bad, but this sound still let him feel how he was connected to the world.

Without his consciously realizing it, all kinds of people's help had gotten him here. If he'd chosen just a slightly different path, if he'd made just one decision differently, his future might have been a lot different than where he was now. Right now, though, he was glad from the bottom of his heart that he'd chosen how he had. He'd gotten sick of it so many times, and he'd tried to cast it aside or run away from it, but he was glad he'd managed to make it here. Right now he could feel genuinely grateful to have met all the people he'd encountered along this path.

"Corporal ... can you hang in there a little further?"

Kshht, answered the noise.

"Yeah ... Let's hang on and do our best."

A little further, a little further.

That's how they'd gotten this far, and that's how the end was truly getting closer now.

CHAPTER 4

ONCE, BACK WHEN SHE WAS HAPPY

I wonder who died.

They were holding a funeral for someone. It was in a large clearing with lots of grave markers made of white stone, all neatly lined up. A crowd of people had gathered there wearing mourning clothes and dark-colored hats. The people all stood with their eyes downcast while the priest in long black robes at the very front of the group gave the eulogy. The low voice in prayer permeated the air in the quiet clearing.

At the end of the line of people were a girl and boy in mourning clothes, standing hand in hand.

Poor things...
I hear the brother and sister were left all alone in the world, is that right?

Hearing their whispers, the girl gripped the sniffling and sobbing boy's hand tightly, biting her lip and dropping her gaze to the ground.

What will they do now? They're just children.
The young lady is pretty, so maybe a rich estate will take her on?

More whispering. Right in the middle of the solemnly continuing funeral, the adults held this inappropriate conversation.

The girl glared down at the golden hair rippling softly over her shoulders, her pride and joy, and looked annoyed. She was in her midteens, and the boy looked right around ten or so; both sported attractive blond hair set off nicely by their black clothes.

Squeezing her little brother's hand hard, the girl lifted her face. Her light ice-blue eyes stared straight ahead, as if to defy anything and everything in this world.

She pitched her voice so that only her brother could hear and whispered coldly, "I'm going to be a soldier. You do your best on your own, too."

When the images blurred away, they revealed an unmoving painting hanging on the wall where they had been. It was of a group of girls in poor farmer's clothes, backs bent as they plowed the dry wilderness. There wasn't a trace of the mid-funeral graveyard scene, or the boy and girl, or the crowd in mourning clothes either.

She rolled over on the bed to face up. The decorative lighting fixtures were turned off now, but she could make out most of their contours against the ceiling.

As she twirled a strand of her golden-blond hair carelessly around her fingertip, she stared up at the ceiling and thought, *I wonder who that was…*

Evidently rumors were springing up here and there that Father Sigri was keeping a beautiful lover at his home in midtown.

This was actually true, but his assistant was fairly certain there was a gap between the reality and the gossip fuel people were thinking of. The "beauty" they talked about was beautiful, sure, but she was what you'd call the Elder's hostage, not his lover (and anyway, officially speaking he was unmarried, so even if he did have a lover, it really shouldn't be an issue), and furthermore, the woman was ridiculously selfish and bossy.

Father Sigri had ordered them to let her do as she pleased and then had been so busy ever since that he hadn't spared her a second thought. And so at this point, his home was in fact run just exactly as she pleased. Thanks to which she'd completely ensconced herself in the Sigri residence, even though she could probably escape if she really tried.

That day, the priest went to visit with a few giant boxes of clothes in his arms.

"Your work is appreciated, sir," said the lone Church Soldier on loan from the Security Forces, with feeling.

"How is she?"

"The same."

"The same?"

"Yes."

The priest and the guard nodded to each other and sighed, very much with feeling.

"I'm coming in," said the priest in perfunctory greeting, shifting his parcels to one arm and using the key to her second-floor room that the Elder had given him. When he opened the door, she turned around from holding up an outfit in front of herself at the huge full-length mirror she'd instructed them to put in her room.

As soon as she saw his face, she shrieked, "You're late!"

"I-I'm sorry," he replied, privately wondering if, as a coward, it was his lot in life to apologize when he didn't see any reason why he should have to.

Her room (because somewhere along the way it had most definitely become *her room*) was in such a sorry state that the phrase "ashes of war" came to mind. The surface of the bed and the entire floor were both so completely covered with new clothes and open boxes that there was quite literally no room to walk without stepping on something. He even saw liquor bottles liberally scattered among it all. "Did you buy them for me?" She ran up to him on her bare feet and forcibly seized the boxes he was holding, then rushed back to her bed and jumped onto it, where she started tearing apart the wrapping excitedly.

"Yes, yes, this is the stuff. It's always best to pair this dress with simple ones like these, you know?"

She fished out the black-enamel stiletto heels he'd scoured the town for, trying to get as close as possible to what she'd ordered. One in each hand, she lifted them up to eye level and examined them critically, cocking her head to one side in apparent dissatisfaction.

"Hmm...now, if the heels were just a centimeter or five taller, I'd have no complaints...Oh, well, I'll compromise. Your taste isn't half-bad. You could net yourself a fine girlfriend."

"Gee, thanks," he sighed. He was relieved that he'd at least passed inspection, but he seriously worried over why he was the one saying thank you. She immediately took her new shoes to the mirror and started pairing them with the black dress she was wearing. Twirling around to face him and actually striking a pose, one hand dramatically sweeping her hair back, she asked, "What do you think?"

"Eh?!"

The priest had never in a million years dreamed he'd be asked to comment. He faltered a bit before venturing, "... Yes, fine."

"What kind of way is that to say it?"

She frowned in displeasure, so he hastily rephrased. "It all suits you. Very much."

He wasn't just saying so. The chic black ensemble that set off her golden hair suited her more than enough for her to host a high-society party without having to change a thing.

She looked like nothing so much as an ordinarily (well, extraordinarily) beautiful, ordinary (extraordinarily selfish, rather) young woman, and yet she was an ultimate weapon of massacre that had killed scores of people back in the War, and people called her the witch that had started the "Great Fire of Toulouse," and she was a wanted woman who'd had a bounty on her head for more than eighty years... Although he certainly didn't want to encourage her to act more like a "weapon of massacre," he couldn't help feeling annoyed by the disconnect. He wondered if her life would have been something very different if only she hadn't been born during the War era.

"Say, listen, don't you think this skirt would be better with more of a slit in it?"

"What?!" *How should I know?* "Ah, yes..." The priest tossed out a random answer, at the same time perhaps just the teensi-est part of him thinking that when it came to slits, more was always better.

"Would you lend me some scissors?"

"I'll have someone bring them up to you later," he agreed, hanging his head in resignation. *She makes me so tired...*

"See, I can only wear clip-ons, because if I pierce my ears the holes just close up on me right away, and I can't get the ear-rings out. Being an Undying is such a pain, you know?" She related this grotesque factoid in such a casual manner, taking off her new clip-ons and turning on all fours on the bed to peer into the mirror, examining the effect. Softly rippling waves of golden hair against a black outfit and earrings with bright coppery stones accentuating both—the woman was already beautiful enough without dressing up, but when she did, she was especially gorgeous.

Tilting her head to cast a glance at her earrings in the mir-ror, she asked him in a breezy voice, "Hey, isn't Kieli here yet?"

"Oh, she's already in town. She's staying at headquarters right now."

As soon as she heard his offhanded answer, she stopped short.

"......Kieli's here?" she asked again, turning to him strangely stiffly.

"That's what I just said. I believe you'll be able to see her soon."

Almost before he finished answering, the shoes she'd been wearing were flying through the air straight for him. "Ack!" Reflex jerked his head backward. The shoes crashed against the doorway behind him. His heart raced in his chest—he'd come *this* close to catching one of those stilettos in the eye. He'd thought he was going to die.

"Wh-what was that for?!"

"Get out!"

He was the one who wanted to take issue with *her*, but with no preamble she started shrieking hysterically. "Get out! Nobody come in here! Just go away!"

"Hey—wah!" Shoes, clothes, boxes, and all manner of things came sailing at the priest, chasing him out of the room before he could even make out what was going on. The door slammed closed behind him immediately after he crossed the threshold. His heart still racing, he pounded on the door and called, "What's the matter with you?"

"Shut up. Don't you dare come in here!" he heard a muffled voice shriek from the other side of the door. She'd been the very picture of a good mood ordering him around like her own personal servant just a few seconds ago, and now she wanted him to "go away"?

What the heck was that about . . . ?

The priest stood dumbstruck in front of the locked door.

I . . . really don't understand women.

※

Loathing them, that despot banished them
to a planet of sand and barren fields
O ye prisoners bound for another planet, plow the wilderness
and grow wheat

*   *   *

She heard a song coming from within the painting. A mother was soothing her baby, who wouldn't stop crying. With her baby in her arms, she looked just like the Holy Mother in all those religious paintings, but this Holy Mother was crooning a parody of the hymn singing God's praises. An old tale that recollected the people who had truly done the service of tilling the wilderness: the prisoners. The ladies-in-waiting frowned at the lyrics, but that didn't seem to bother her at all.

The child wrapped in a white baby blanket in her mother's arms still wouldn't stop crying. Her mother began speaking to her tenderly. "There's nothing to be scared of. There's nothing to be scared of anymore, is there? Look, the scary people are gone, and the birdies have come instead." When she pointed into the empty air, the baby gradually went from sobbing to a soft fretting, and then her tear-streaked face began to beam. Soon she was squealing with laughter. She waved both tiny hands lightly in the air as if trying to chase something flying there.

Wave, wave. The baby's young hands and dark eyes roamed the empty space.

And then her wide-eyed gaze swiveled this way.

Deeply dark, jet-black eyes.

You betrayed me, didn't you . . . In a hoarse voice like an old woman's, the baby said, *You talked, didn't you . . . If* you'd *kept your mouth shut, nobody would have known. How dare you sell me out...*

The baby's black eyes started turning around and around madly, and then maggots began crawling out of both of them in thick droves. Slowly and steadily, more and more of them squirmed out of the painting and over its frame, spreading out over the wall. Even the people in the other paintings around them began to follow suit, cackling. *You sold out your friend. She would never betray you, and yet you betrayed her...*

"Shut up! Go away! Don't come out of there!" she shrieked, and threw a shoe. The heel made a mark in the wall, then fell to the floor. The room around her abruptly quieted.

With her throwing arm still raised, she froze in place for a while, breathing raggedly. In the dull glow of the overhead light, the paintings were back to normal; the baby and the picture frame and the wall that had all been covered in maggots were gone, as was the taunting laughter. The people in the paintings were back to still figures at the plow.

Her throat had gone dry. She slid unsteadily out of bed, wanting water.

When she walked past the mirror in the center of the room, she caught a glimpse of her own profile reflected back at her.

Hee-hee...

The Beatrix in the mirror gave a giggle. No sooner had Beatrix turned back toward the mirror, pale-faced, than the self in the glass burst into shrill laughter. Her face's reflection in the mirror twisted unpleasantly.

"Stop pretending to be me!" she shrieked hysterically.

"What are you talking about? I *am* you." The mirror laughed madly.

"I said stop! You just drop dead!"

"Go ahead and kill me, if you can. You're me. I can't die."

"Shut up!"

Holding up the shoe she'd automatically picked up from the floor, this time Beatrix hurled it at the mirror. With a snap, cracks ran through the mirror in a circle around the center where it had hit, but she could still hear the laughter coming from somewhere, not stopping. "You should just die. It's not like there's any fun waiting for you if you live. You can dress yourself up in these silly clothes, but it'll only make you feel empty. You should just die, if you can. I mean, you're tired of it all now, aren't you...?"

In the cracked mirror, her own hideously deformed face kept on cackling and cackling and cackling, egging her on.

You should just die. You should just die.

Father Sigri had left the priest in charge of his home (practically left him to his own devices there, actually) and told him to use whatever things in the house he needed, so whenever he visited he helped himself to the coffee and brewed himself a cup for a little break before he went home. It was a modest house overall, but coffee was the one thing its owner had splurged on. It was quite good stuff.

Incidentally, Father Sigri had dislocated his shoulder the previous night tripping down the stairs or some such thing, and the Council of Elders, which was presently down from eleven men to six, was frowning on him for getting himself hurt when they were so shorthanded. Apparently those old men didn't have the imagination to harbor the same basic doubt he did, which was whether Father Sigri could really have managed to dislocate his shoulder from a simple tumble down the steps.

Hey, look what I found.

Casually peeking into the living room cabinets, he discovered a bottle of brandy. Although Church doctrine didn't prohibit alcohol, it did tend to prescribe moderation. However, he know Father Sigri had a habit of taking brandy in his coffee, so he got a little urge to try it out himself.

Although this house was very modest for someone of its owner's lineage and status, to the young priest, who had naturally never owned his own home, the sofa in the living room was plenty luxurious. He sank his body into the choicest part of it and sipped his brandied coffee like the very Father himself.

...... This really doesn't taste good.

It was a bizarre flavor: bitterness multiplied by more bitterness. He couldn't fathom why the man drank this stuff voluntarily. Now that he thought about it, he wasn't sure he'd ever seen Father Sigri wear a pleasant look on his face while he drank it. Aside from the brandied coffee ritual that must be some sort of ascetic practice, the only impressions of the Father in his mind were of him constantly working.

He'd tried playing high-society man, but all it did was... make him feel kind of empty.

He was putting his cup down with a sigh when a sudden

CRASH from overhead sent him reflexively leaping to his feet. His heart leaping along with the rest of him, he burst out of the room to see what was happening. "M-Mr. Yoshiu!" called the guard in a panic, leaning over the railing of the second-floor hall. He ran up the stairs, joined the guard, and dashed to her room. When he reached the doorway, shock brought him up short.

She was standing in the middle of the room in front of the mirror, a pair of scissors raised in one hand. The mirror had cracks in it like the spokes of a wheel, and shards of glass lay scattered everywhere. Too late, he realized his mistake. She hadn't shown any signs of dangerous behavior recently (setting the selfishness aside), and he'd let his guard down far enough to hand her *scissors*, of all things—which was obviously beyond the limits of what it was permissible to allow a hostage.

A section of her soft blond curls was lopped off just below the chin, lying in tufts at her feet. Her formerly beautiful hair-cut was half-butchered horribly. A stream of blood poured from her neck.

"Wh-what are you doing?!" he called from where he stood faltering in the doorway. She turned sluggishly toward him with a vaguely unsettled gaze. The blood flowing from her neck was dyeing her pale slip a bright red, but the blood around the cut itself had transformed into a black liquid like coal tar and was already beginning to close the wound.

"I can't die..." she said, tilting her head as if this confused her.

"W-well, obviously! I mean, not that that would normally be obvious!" *What am I even saying?!*

"Aha-ha!"

Without warning, she burst out laughing and dropped the scissors to the floor with a clatter.

"Ahaha, hahaha, hohohohaha..."

As the priest and guard looked on in horror, she crumpled weakly to the hair- and glass-covered floor like a puppetmaster's doll after its strings had been cut and just kept on laughing and laughing in a toneless, scratchy voice just like a broken doll.

It was Kieli's fifth day in the capital when she was allowed to see Beatrix. That priest named Yoshiu who was acting as her caretaker took her out to Father Sigri's private residence in one of the capital's ordinary residential districts. When Kieli suspiciously asked the priest why she had permission to see Beatrix all of a sudden, the priest answered in his usual half-fearful way. "You see, she's beyond our control...I'll tell you right now: We didn't do anything to her, all right?" Kieli didn't really understand what he was talking about, but it sounded rather like some sort of excuse.

Father Sigri's residence was a surprisingly normal house. It was more than fancy enough by Kieli's standards, of course, but it wasn't garishly overembellished either. It was probably a lot humbler than the high priest of Easterbury parish's house.

"This is the house where you were born, you know."

Kieli hadn't registered that aspect of things until she heard him say it.

She put a hand on the railing of the staircase, feeling a tangle of different emotions. It was cool and well polished; it seemed to fit her hand. There were almost no decorations, but she saw a relatively large number of paintings on the walls and wondered where that touch had come from. Was it Father Sigri, or did that show her mother's tastes?

Whee!

Thinking she heard a whooping child run by behind her, Kieli turned. But there was nothing there other than the thin sandy sunbeams filtering into the entryway and the paintings on the walls.

Lots of things live in this house, huh...

Up the stairs across from the entrance was a semicircular corridor. The priest unlocked the door to a room on one side all the way at the far end.

"She might be dangerous, so please be careful," the priest warned as he half-shoved Kieli into the doorway. Something about him gave her the impression that he was ready to run away any second.

Kieli's heart pounded violently. Ever since they'd ended up parting after that fight at the bar on the parish border, she'd missed Beatrix so much, and she'd wanted to apologize, and she'd been so worried all along for her safety. She wanted to make up with her and talk about lots of things. So much had happened since then; she wanted Beatrix to listen to all of it. Kieli just knew she hadn't changed a bit, and she'd get exasperated and say *What are you, an idiot?* and be sarcastic at her sometimes, but all the while she'd be listening to Kieli sympathetically. Kieli wanted to talk to her about Harvey and the Corporal, too. She couldn't handle all her unease on her own anymore, but she knew she could go to Beatrix about it.

Now she finally got to see her. *Beatrix—*

The curtains were drawn and the room was poorly lit. Kieli's eyes had adjusted to the natural light in the entryway; now a sort of greenish afterimage seemed burned into her field of vision, and she couldn't make anything out right away. As her vision adjusted, she gasped at the state of the room.

Cast-off garments and clothes boxes and liquor bottles were scattered every which way all over the room. Several of the paintings on the walls were askew, and several more had come unhooked and crashed to the floor. Shards of a broken mirror lay strewn in the very center of the room.

O ye prisoners bound for another planet, plow the wilderness…

Kieli heard a light crooning that didn't really jell together into a melody coming from the bed. There was someone lying in the bed. Her golden hair was hacked off unevenly on one side and hardened into clumps by the blood covering it; her slip was stained rust-red and immodestly disarranged, the hem barely covering her at the bottom and the straps falling off her shoulders; she was singing brokenly, sometimes breaking into abrupt giggles; and she waved her slim fingers lightly in the air in a drunken circle-like shape.

The unsteady singing permeated the dimness of the room.

"Beatrix...?" Kieli called in a raspy voice.

Beatrix's eyes roamed the air—she was still singing under her breath—before turning in this direction. Kieli waited nervously until after a beat she drawled, "So, who are you? A new maid?"

"Beatrix," Kieli said again, a little lower this time, but in a clearer voice.

At that call, Beatrix's finger stopped short where it had been drawing aimless circles in the air, and the woman's eyes turned toward her again, this time properly looking. Her blue eyes blinked hard once, then twice. The beautiful woman with the ice-blue eyes hadn't changed a bit, and fondness swelled in Kieli's heart. She'd missed her for so long and wanted to apologize...

"Beatrix...!" She started to run toward her, eyes swimming.

"Get out!"

What looked like a slipper came flying through the air straight for her. Kieli couldn't dodge in time, and it scraped past her cheek to hit the priest standing behind her square in the face. He cried out even louder than Kieli had. "Wh-what?!" There wasn't even a split second for Kieli to grasp the situation before clothes and boxes and everything else Beatrix could get her hands on were hurled violently her way. Peeling off the skirt or whatever it was that had landed on her head, Kieli said, "Beatrix! Wh-what's gotten into you?"

"Get out! Go on, get out!"

Objects were fired in her direction at random until she couldn't take it anymore and retreated temporarily to the shadow of the doorway. As soon as she peeked back inside, guarding her head with her arm, the other slipper hurtled toward her. Batting away the slipper as it struck her arm, Kieli cried, "Beatrix, come on, it's me! What's wrong?"

"You came to get mad and yell at me, right? Don't lie to me; I know you did!"

"Yell at you...? What are you talking about?"

"Look out!"

In the same instant that the priest grabbed her by the arm and yanked her back, a pair of scissors embedded itself blades-first into the doorjamb she'd been peering around just a split second ago. *That* made a chill run up her spine. For a moment, Beatrix stopped in her tracks, looking surprised herself.

Kieli took advantage of that momentary window to shake off the priest's hands and dash into the room. Beatrix, apparently afraid of her, pulled a blanket over her head and burrowed beneath the bedclothes. Kieli heard a muffled voice from one end of the blanket shout, "Stay away! I said *stay away*!"

"What...?"

Beatrix was misbehaving and making a scene like a little kid. For a short while Kieli stood still at the bedside, flabbergasted. She'd worried like crazy, and she'd been so excited to finally meet her again, her heart racing as she'd come all the way out here, and now... She slowly began to feel an actual swell of rage in her chest. "What the heck does that mean? I don't even understand what you're saying! Let's really talk about this, Beatrix!"

"No!"

Beatrix shrieked and fought back as Kieli tried to rip away the blanket. *This is just crazy.* Now Kieli was starting to want to cry, too. *Why are we playing tug-of-war like little kids?!*

Beatrix's hand grazed her cheek, trying to yank the blanket back, and one nail gouged away a tiny bit of skin. "Ow!" Kieli blurted softly, and then Beatrix cried out, a little surprised "Ah—" too. They both stopped moving for a moment and stared at each other.

Kieli bit her lip hard.

Whack!

She slapped Beatrix back hard on the cheek. Beatrix stayed there, frozen, gaping at Kieli as though she couldn't process the fact that she'd been slapped.

"Wh-why…" Panting heavily, Kieli gasped out, "Why are we—why are we doing this? It's stupid! I'm mad! Yeah, I'm mad! I worried about you for so long, and I missed you, a-and I've felt just as alone as you ever since I got here…! And now—what—what is this?! You've been buying up all the clothes in town and getting drunk and throwing stuff everywhere and not even caring how I felt all this time?!" The tears finally spilled over; she couldn't hold out anymore. She felt stupid and ridiculous and pathetic for crying through her shouting like this, but that only made it harder to stop.

Still hugging the blanket to her chest, Beatrix gaped at her.

"Aren't you…aren't you mad at me for telling them about you…?" she asked, sounding nervous. This time it was Kieli's turn to gape, tears still streaming down her face.

"Huh? Why would I be mad?"

"B-because then they dragged you out here, right?! Then you couldn't look for Ephraim! I-I just kind of didn't care about anything anymore, and I told them everything about you without thinking about it, and then I heard they were going to go get you, and I realized I'd really blown it, and I felt bad, but it was too late…" Her face was a crumpled mess as she talked, and soon she was wailing like a toddler, too. "I'm sorry, I'm so sorry…"

"What are you talking about? I did find Harvey. I got to see him. Harvey's been worried about you all this time, too, you know. And the Corporal, too! We were all worried, okay?"

When Kieli hugged her golden head in both hands where the hair that had been her point of pride was so painfully shaggy now and drew her face close, Beatrix blinked at her with tear-filled eyes.

"You got to see Ephraim…?"

"Yeah, I did. I really did."

Beatrix's eyes widened in disbelief, and then she started sobbing again, soaking her face even more with tears. "Oh. That's good…that's really good…"

"Yeah. Yeah." Kieli nodded, crying herself. They both leaned in close, until they bumped foreheads.

"What were you thinking, doing this to your hair? This is such a waste! What are you, an idiot?!" Kieli said, delivering the same line she'd expected to hear from Beatrix sort of angrily through her tears. Then Beatrix got angry through her own tears the same way and cried, "You're the one who's an idiot! This is all *your* fault for running off without telling anyone!"

"That was because *you* lied to me!"

The glared at each other, both scowling. The priest was standing petrified in the doorway of the room, as if he just couldn't make any response to these two girls crying one minute and quarreling the next.

They held each other's glares for several seconds.

And then...

"Aaaa!"

"Aaaaaaa, Beatrix!"

Their faces both crumpled again and they started clutching each other and sobbing without a scrap of dignity. They cried and cried until they'd cried themselves out. When Kieli cradled Beatrix's head of disheveled hair, the scent of perfumed oil wafted from it, mixed with the faint scent of blood. It was the same old Beatrix scent, and it really hadn't changed at all.

❧

"And listen to this! What do you think he said the first time he saw my face? He said 'Who are you?'!"

"Aha-ha, that sounds just like him."

"Hey, it's not funny!"

Kieli gave a look of real hurt, which Beatrix laughed off without constraint.

She told Beatrix all about the things that had happened since she'd left the bar on her own and headed for Gate Town, sometimes in order, sometimes jumping back and forth. Lounging on the big bed together hugging pillows, almost like roommates staying up at night chatting, somehow. There was a guard outside the room, and for Kieli this was still smack-dab in the middle of enemy territory, and they couldn't contact Harvey or the Corporal...She had heaps of problems, but for the first time since she'd come to the capital, she felt at ease.

"And he forgot my birthday again when I turned seventeen, too! I mean, do you remember what happened back in South-hairo? He forgot my birthday the year I first met you, too, and wandered off somewhere…" Before she knew it, she was rattling off more of her mounting pile of grievances, increasingly bad-mouthing Harvey. As soon as she started talking about birthdays, though, Beatrix took on a stupefied look.

"…You forgot, too, didn't you, Beatrix? And you said you'd celebrate it with me this year, too!"

When Kieli gave her a look dripping with suspicion, Beatrix cried, "Wh-what?! No, no, of course I remembered!" in obvious panic, flopped down on the mattress with a thump, and began doing something or other with her hands. "Wait just a second." Since they'd ended up lying with their heads pointed in opposite directions, Kieli had a view of Beatrix's bare feet and couldn't see her face.

"What are you doing?"

"No peeking."

"Hmph."

Kieli lifted her head and tried to peek, and got a pillow thrown in her face for it. "Sheesh," she huffed, flumping back down in the bed again. It had been so long since she'd spent time unwinding like this that a comfortable sleepiness came over her. She hadn't really been able to get much sleep during her stay at the Preaching Department tower.

O ye prisoners bound for another planet, plow the wilderness and grow wheat

And then God shall appear
All the land belongs to God, wheat is an offering unto God

Beatrix's soft crooning reached Kieli's ears as she started to nod off. It was the same song she'd been singing earlier. Dozing with one cheek pressed to the pillow, Kieli listened to her clear voice. She wasn't sure why, but the more she listened, the more she felt a dim pang of nostalgia. *It's almost as if someone sang this for me once, a long time ago...*

"What song is that? I feel like I've heard it before..."

Prisoners bound for another planet—Harvey had once told her that the ones who'd developed this planet's wilderness weren't believers like the holy book taught; they were prisoners sent here back when this was an exile planet, long before the Church was established here.

Harvey...

Unease flickered again in her heart as she remembered him.

...But I know he'll come, no matter what...

When she'd brought it up with Beatrix, her friend had been confident. *He said he'd come to get you, right? "No matter what." So he'll come.* Kieli hadn't known how Beatrix could be so completely sure about that, and she hadn't been able to wipe away the worry. When her expression stayed gloomy, Beatrix poked her forehead and laughed a little. *He isn't the kind of guy who uses self-confident words like that. Ever. To the point where it's a pain in the ass for the rest of us.* (Kieli had to admit that she had a point there.) *He said "no matter what," and he says that about once every six blue moons, so he'll come, no matter what.*

Kieli clung to those words, shutting her eyes and clasping her hands in front of her chest almost in prayer.

"Kieli, give me your arm."

She opened her eyes at the sound of Beatrix's voice. The woman had still been working on something while Kieli thought, and her feet were still the first thing to greet Kieli's eyes. Then, without getting up, she wriggled around like a sandworm until her head was facing the same direction as Kieli's. Kieli stared blankly as Beatrix took her arm and tied something around her wrist.

"Hmm? What's this?"

"A good-luck charm. It's your birthday present. It's to make sure you get to see Ephraim... and this thing seriously answers prayer, you know! Because it's got my vengeful undead hatred in it." She proclaimed this with proud satisfaction. *I'd rather you didn't put your vengeful hatred in it, though*... Lifting her left hand in front of her, Kieli stared with wide eyes at the bracelet-like thing tied around her wrist. A copper-colored stone apparently torn from one of Beatrix's earrings dangled from a cord braided out of strands of her chopped-off blond hair.

"Th-thanks... I like it. It's handmade..."

Her eyes still smarted from crying them out earlier, but they started tearing up anyway. She couldn't even remember the last time she'd gotten a birthday present, let alone a hand-made one.

She'd been thrilled when she said her thanks, but Beatrix scowled unhappily anyway. "Well, excuse me for giving you something handmade. I never spend money on presents for people, okay?! It's a matter of policy," she said, as if that was something to brag about for some reason. Kieli burst out laughing with the tears still in her eyes. Laughing and crying, she squeezed her other hand tightly around the charm and the wrist it was tied around.

"Okay, then I'll give you something, too!"

Kieli flipped over and edged closer to her, pressing her forehead to Beatrix's. Beatrix blinked.

"You don't need to give anything. It's not *my* birthday."

"Then I'm giving you something on your next birthday, no matter what! On the day in the middle of summer."

"... You just decided that day on your own!" Beatrix said, her cheek twitching, but then her expression relaxed and she smiled tolerantly. "Well, not that I mind."

"Then let's definitely celebrate. It's a promise, okay?"

"Okay, okay."

"You promise. No matter what."

"No matter what."

Lying on the bed, they pressed their foreheads together and agreed on it.

Now, Kieli believed in the words "no matter what." Maybe there weren't really any "no matter whats" in this world, but right now, she believed that there were with all her heart.

She hadn't felt so at ease during the night in a long time. Not long after that conversation, before many more words had even been spoken, Kieli fell asleep next to her friend. There were lots and lots of things left she wanted to talk about, but all of a sudden the sleepiness swept over her.

But that was okay. She knew that even if she slept tonight,

they could talk again tomorrow, and the day after that, and whenever they wanted, from now on.

"O ye prisoners bound for another planet, plow the wilderness..."

They'd infected him with the song. The priest shrugged hopelessly at himself when he caught himself murmuring it softly and shut his mouth.

It was the middle of the night, in a corner of a half-lit hallway. Slumped next to the door of their room, he sipped his now stone-cold brandied coffee. The singing and talking he'd heard coming from inside all night was gone now, and a late-night hush had begun to sink over the house.

"Mr. Yoshiu, singing that...might not be the best idea," the soldier standing at attention on the opposite side of the door murmured hesitantly. He continued to face forward. The priest likewise faced forward, sipping at his coffee and smiling wryly as he murmured back, "Yes, you're right..."

They were parody lyrics that criticized the Church's teachings. If anyone were to overhear him, he'd suffer worse than a few scowls—they might even treat him like a heretic. And yet...he couldn't help thinking these lyrics were more interesting.

"Mr. Yoshiu. What do you suppose we're doing here?" the guard asked, in the same quiet voice.

This time the priest was the one to warn him off as he gazed vaguely through the railing at a painting hanging in the entryway. "...That's a question best not to ask out loud."

And this time it was the guard's turn to say, "You're right…"

They're just two young ladies, just two close friends who went in search of each other after missing each other for a long time; why should I have to stand guard over them like this? He didn't have enough conviction or drive to go against his orders, however.

……It really doesn't taste good.

The cold brandied coffee on his tongue definitely had a bizarre flavor. Just like bitter, uncooperative reality, somehow.

❧

She saw a tidy little white house in the painting. It looked just like a finely detailed painting itself. A house, a front garden with snug little flower beds, and a picket fence. A bomber plane roared across the sky overhead, but the little house sat there as peacefully as if it had no connection at all to that violent world.

"Siiisssss!" a little boy called, on the verge of tears. A young girl came out of the house. The boy and the girl were both much younger than that time they'd worn mourning clothes. She wore a light green pinafore; he wore shorts and a vest of the same green. In the branches of the tree he pointed at, whining, was a toy…ae-ro-plane?…that had gotten stuck.

Airplane. Yes—this was back when their planet still had the energy to power "airplanes."

"Right, here I go," said the girl, looking up at the garden tree and hitching up the hem of her pinafore.

"Sis, that's dangerous!"

"Nah, I'll be fine!"

She began fearlessly climbing the tree right in front of her agitated little brother and reached out toward the branch the airplane was caught on. No sooner had she cried "Got it!" than the branch she was gripping for balance broke. There was a series of snaps and rattles and crashes, and the little brother started wailing loudly. Just then a car pulled up to the curb in front of the house, and their parents leapt out of the car at the sound of him, faces pale with fear.

"Ow, ow, ow..."

By the time the girl hastily sat up, holding a hand to the back of her head, she was surrounded by worried-looking family members on all sides. In her hand was the airplane. She'd kept hold of it the whole time, never dropping it in the fall. "Sorry..." she said, shrinking a little in embarrassment. As one, the family heaved a sigh of relief. The girl shoved the airplane into her little brother's hands as he blubbered her name and told him coldly, "No crying. Boys don't cry." He still sniffled, but he wiped the tears fiercely away so she wouldn't scold him.

The girl dropped her gaze. "Aw, man..."

There was a huge tear in the hem of her skirt where it had snagged on a tree branch. When she lifted it up, she exposed a scratch along the skin of her bare leg.

"Sorry... I tore it."

She looked up apologetically at her parents, who exchanged amused glances.

"Well, good timing."

As the girl gaped at that, her father fetched a giant clothing box from the car. "Happy birthday."

The girl's eyes widened when he presented it to her. It was so big, she couldn't get her young arms all the way around it. She'd completely forgotten that it was her birthday today. She practically ripped the box open, delighted at the unexpected gift, and found an adorable snow-white dress inside. It was just a little more grown-up than the ones she had, and it really hit her that she was a year older now.

"Thank you!"

Holding her new outfit up in front of her with both hands, she hopped around the garden with complete disregard for the scrapes on her legs. Her parents called to her to wait until later or she'd get it dirty, but they were watching the whole thing with wry smiles. The little boy chased his sister around as she ran. The family's laughter echoed in the garden.

Happy birthday, Beatrix.

Happy birthday, Bea. Sis—

When the image faded out, the painting had gone back to the same old still picture of people tilling the wilderness. The room was quiet; she couldn't hear the voice of that horrible her in the mirror or the cackles of the ghosts in the paintings. Just the soft, calm breathing of the girl sleeping next to her.

She got up and sat on the edge of the bed to look up at what she could see of the painting in the dimness.

Sheesh…

A single tear slid down her cheek.

Happy birthday, Bea. Sis—

*　　*　　*

The bright voices sprang back to life in her mind.

That's me. That girl's me. So, even she'd been happy once, surrounded by her family. There'd been a time when she was happy, with people who protected her and things she wanted to protect.

If what reminded me just now was the whim of some sort of force, like what you could call the planet's god…

I'll say "thanks," just in case.

I was plenty happy.

In the morning, the sound of broken glass once again had him jumping up from the sofa, where he'd been snoozing. He really wished they would stop doing this. It was bad for his heart. When he burst out of the first-floor living room, the guard leaned over the railing of the second-floor hall exactly like before and shouted, "Mr. Yoshiu, outside!"

The priest turned away from the stairs and flew past the entryway to jump straight out into the front garden, upon which he immediately skidded to a stop, doubting his own eyes.

Two girls were falling down from the second-story window—!

A blond woman landed on the ground with a raven-haired girl hanging around her neck. She wobbled a little on the landing, but other than that, she caught the girl in her arms and deposited her on the ground without any particular sign of danger. "Phew, I'm a little out of shape," she said, cracking her neck and looking irritatingly self-satisfied.

The girl, on the other hand, was pale-faced. "That was crazy, Beatrix!"

"We landed safely, so what's the problem?" The blonde pouted, like this was so unreasonable.

They didn't get very far before they came to a stop in front of the priest, who had unwittingly blocked their path through the garden. Behind the untidy blond hair falling in her face, the woman grinned, hooked one arm around the girl's neck, and pressed a pair of scissors to her throat.

"Huh?!" The girl looked blindsided. Though the priest flinched, he somehow managed not to lose his nerve; instead, he spread both arms out wide in front of them.

"I-I'm not going to fall for that! It's plain as day you're just acting!"

His voice rang somewhat hollow in his own ears. Unperturbed, she said, "So what? The point is, you had no choice but to let me go, because I took your boss's daughter hostage. You follow me?"

"...Huh?"

"If you'd rather get beaten up, that's fine, too," she told him with a highly disturbing smile. *That* was enough to give him cold feet. He gulped. The guard finally burst into the garden. But Yoshiu turned his outspread hands toward him and gestured for him to halt. The woman giggled and tugged on the girl's hand.

"I've got some business to take care of, so I'm off. Well, then...you made life here a little bearable. Thanks."

She left him with a first-class wink that shot straight through his heart even in *this* situation, turning on her heel and leaving him and the guard both frozen to the spot. They could only stand there and watch them kick open the garden gate and disappear. (The woman literally kicked the gate—and hard; the hinges came clean off.)

"Wh-what should we do, Mr. Yoshiu?"

"Um…" The priest was still staring off in the direction they'd disappeared when he answered the guard. "At times like these, the first thing is to notify our superiors."

Thank goodness they both happened to have superiors who weren't too cruel, the two men agreed with feeling.

They finally stopped running when they reached a patch of high ground overlooking the pedestrian bridge over the railroad tracks, where they could see a long line of pilgrims making their way up the sloping path to Church headquarters. They'd sprinted the whole way through midtown, so Kieli was completely out of breath. Beatrix, meanwhile, looked just fine. Kieli glared at her a little enviously.

"You scared me there," she complained. "For a second I thought you were serious!"

"Well, I would have been, depending on what he did," Beatrix tossed back breezily, shoving the scissors she was carrying at Kieli. Kieli looked down at them blankly.

"Will you cut it for me?"

She shook her disordered hair lightly at Kieli. When Kieli widened her eyes in astonishment, she said, "Just look at how awful it looks now. I'd be better off going short." She smiled, carefree, as if it didn't trouble her at all. "Then let's go blend in with them. We look perfect for it."

Beatrix pointed at the long, snakelike line of pilgrims below them. Kieli and Beatrix were both wearing black clothes, so if they slipped into that procession of people in dark greatcoats and hats, they should blend right in. Off in the distance, Kieli could see where they were headed: the dark-gray spires of the Church headquarters.

"It's okay," Beatrix reassured her when she saw the uneasy expression on Kieli's face as she gazed at those faraway towers. Her waist-length hair had been beautiful, of course, but this shaggy, uneven hair really suited her frank personality, too. Beatrix was always beautiful and strong.

"If he's coming, I think he'll head straight for headquarters. It's okay. You'll get to see him."

"...Yeah."

Kieli nodded and gripped the good-luck charm around her left wrist hard. A copper-colored stone against Beatrix's blond hair: the best charm there could be, made out of the colors Kieli loved best. Harvey, the Corporal...and Joachim, who hadn't shown himself since that time in the hallway. How were they all now?

It's okay. I know everything will go fine, and we can all go home together.

She squeezed the bracelet with her right hand, tightly balling her left hand into a fist, too, and stared hard straight ahead at the headquarters they were headed for.

CHAPTER 5
WHAT LIES AT THE END OF THE WORLD

Hey, what kind of person is God?

Julius had once asked his nursemaid that, too. As a small child he really had had an endless need to know things; he wouldn't rest until he'd cleared up whatever question was bothering him.

Hmm ... I've never met Him either, you know, she'd answered, looking sort of at a loss.

I wonder if all the really important people have met Him!

Yes, I suppose they must have. The Elders receive the word of God directly, after all. You might get to be an Elder someday, too, you know.

Little Julius's eyes lit up at that. *If I got to meet God, I'd ask him for all kinds of stuff! I'd wish for some rare trading cards, and to be stronger, oh, and I want a pet dog! Oh, and then ...*

When he started listing one wish after another, his nurse-maid smiled at him wryly and said, *Now, now, young master, God isn't someone who grants wishes. God is someone who watches over us, loves us, and forgives us.*

R-really ...?

Yes, really.

Oh ... At her explanation, all the excitement of a moment ago vanished, and young Julius hung his head dejectedly. *And I had a bunch more wishes, too ... like for Mom and Dad and you to always like me, and ... for there to be no people in trouble on our planet and for nobody to be sad or hungry or freezing anymore.*

But I guess God doesn't grant wishes like that, huh ...?

I don't need God. "God" never does anything for us.

*　　*　　*

Her words springing to his mind again were like a heavy blow to the chest.

The upper ranks of the Church were trying to deal with both the string of Elder deaths and the monster affair without letting them become widely known. With the Council of Elders still short-staffed, administrative functions at the top were a mess. They had their hands full keeping up appearances to make sure the confusion didn't show; there was currently no official position on the monster issue. Even though civilians were dying. Considering that the Undying Hunters were on the move, it seemed clear that the Council of Elders was somehow involved, or at the very least had information on the monsters, but that information still hadn't come down to the Security Forces, the ones actually attempting to protect the city.

No matter how he tried, Julius couldn't ignore the fact that his distrust in the Church was growing every day. He wanted to believe that his fears were groundless. And yet...

The day it happened, the cold was still unremitting, even though it was just about time for them to be welcoming spring, and the skies were leaden. After receiving a peremptory call that consisted of "Come get me," Julius had come to a train station near headquarters that shuttled people affiliated with the Church. He saw the train pulling up, and then a short time later a gaggle of passengers poured out of the station house, looking somehow more restless than usual.

In a crowd dominated by people in the black greatcoats and hats of the clergy, it wasn't too difficult to spot the tall redhead.

When he stopped in front of the man amid the flow of pass-ersby, the first words out of Julius's mouth were, "It's not a good look on you."

"Shut up."

The redhead who glared grumpily down at him, still mad-deningly half a head taller than he was, wore jet-black priest's robes and a greatcoat with the hood pulled down low over his forehead so that he at least stood out less than usual. Around his neck hung an ancient portable radio Julius recognized. Though a careful observer might notice that the right sleeve tucked in his pocket was empty, at a glance from a distance he looked like any priest coming home from rounds in the coun-try. Apparently, Julius's old nursemaid's husband, who worked at a Security Forces outpost in Gate Town (and whom Julius was fairly close to; he thought of the man as a sort of favorite uncle), had hooked him up with the outfit.

You'd think that the long, high-collared robes themselves would suit his tall, lean form, but he was projecting a decid-edly "outlaw" atmosphere that, as far as Julius was concerned, made the overall effect just wrong. Nobody would take him for anything but a rogue delinquent priest. *I'd look a hundred times handsomer than him in those robes. Probably.* He was willing to bet there wasn't a respectable priest in this world sporting mismatched eyes and a blatantly sketchy sore on his cheek the color and texture of iron rust...

This guy was missing another body part every time Julius saw him.

With some hesitation, he asked, "What happened with your eye?"

"It's a badge of honor."

The other man smirked. Julius fumed. He'd been nice and asked out of *concern*, and he got the feeling he'd been teased for his trouble.

"Yeah, right! That's pathetic, not cool."

"Yup, I'm fighting a lot of losing battles right now, so I'm pretty pathetic." The easy admission struck Julius speechless. *Wow, I don't remember him being so honest and open...* "I don't have time to worry about appearances right now, so I'm just gonna use whatever I can. I called you because getting your help was the most convenient way to do this. Even though I'd really rather shoot myself than owe *you* a favor."

"......"

Never mind, I hate him after all. Julius pursed his lips in disappointment. More than two years had passed since they'd first met on the Sand Ocean, and Julius felt that he'd personally matured at least two years' worth in that time, but just like this guy hadn't gotten older, his messed-up personality really hadn't changed a bit.

A broad connecting bridge extended from the station exit toward Church headquarters. They slipped into the flow of similarly attired people around them and began walking down it side by side.

"...Where's Kieli?"

They were both facing forward when the soft question came. Julius had no doubt he'd been dying to ask that from the very beginning. He *hmph*ed irritably and answered, "I heard she went to Father Sigri's house to meet with the hostage."

"So she got together with Bea..." the other man murmured,

relieved. The way he glanced down at the radio at his chest as he spoke made it look for all the world as though he and the radio were nodding to each other.

"You want to go there?"

"Nah...if she managed to meet up with Bea, we don't have to hurry. First—" He abruptly slowed down and veered a little unsteadily toward one side of the bridge, so Julius followed him warily.

"What's going on?"

"A little smoke break."

"Excuse me?!" To his amazement, the man proceeded to lean on the parapet of the bridge and light up a cigarette under the cover of his hood. "Didn't you just say we don't have time?"

"I don't. So"—he took a deep drag and exhaled—"I gotta dope up with nicotine now, or I'll be dead on my feet before we're done." He didn't sound as if he was joking. Letting the parapet of the bridge support his weight, practically hanging over it as he breathed out his smoke, he did look genuinely in pain. Julius could see now that he was hanging on to his strength of will by a thread, feeding it by being provocative because it was the only thing keeping him on his feet.

"So, about the monster thing."

"Right."

Julius ended up leaning his own back against the parapet next to Harvey and taking a break with him as they spoke. The people coming and going on the bridge glanced their way every so often, but Harvey was facing away from the flow of traffic, so he didn't get any dirty looks for the smoking.

"Can the lab be infiltrated? They have to be coming from there."

"I think we could set it up if we wanted," Julius answered briskly. "At this point I wouldn't mind going to my father about it, but I got a lead from one of my own connections, so—" He broke off when Harvey stopped smoking to blink and stare at him out of the corner of his eye. Julius tensed reflexively, figuring he was about to get teased again. "Wh-what?"

"What you're about to do is treachery. Do you get that?"

"That's a fine thing to say when you're the one who asked me for help."

"I'm not going to force you. I can take you hostage and manage something on my own."

If that's not "force," Julius wondered, *what is?*

"I'm kidding."

"Liar."

"Yup. I'm serious."

"......"

After a bit of reflection, Julius dropped his gaze to his feet and said solemnly, "I just want to know the truth, that's all. I want to know whether what I've believed in all this time, what I've never doubted, was really there... Whether maybe there was never anything there at all..." Had God really been in the place that he'd had his eyes on all this time, that he'd been aiming for all this time?

I don't need God. "God" never does anything for us, Kieli's voice said in the back of his mind.

"Doesn't the Church exist to help people...?"

"…Are you asking *me* whether this world needs the Church? What do you want me to say? My answer's obvious."

It hurt to have his honestly dejected question smacked down like that, but Julius realized that he'd been the insensitive one for asking it, so he couldn't make any retort. To an Undying on the run from the Church, the Church's God was the enemy; obviously he wouldn't need it.

I don't need God—

But…was that really true, though?

"I still don't think the Church is unnecessary, even now. After the War ended and this planet's cities were plagued with starvation and plundering, it was the Church that gave them food, built them heating, and helped restore order. That's—*that's* really true, if nothing else. I've always wanted to be able to help the planet like that, too…" But right now what Julius had aspired to was shrouded in a gray haze, and he couldn't see it so well anymore. What was it that he'd believed in all this time?

The man next to him only gazed casually with his mismatched eyes over the parapet at the city sprawling below them and puffed on his cigarette. Julius didn't even know whether he was listening or not. It wasn't as if he could expect an answer anyway. And he hadn't said those things hoping for one, really, but in the end he still ended up hoping for some kind of response, at least.

Silence fell for a while. The restless flow of people on the connecting bridge continued without pause.

"Julius," his companion said. Julius, who'd long since given up on getting a reaction from him, waited nervously to see what would come next.

"Do you seriously think you can save all the people on this planet?" Harvey asked, as though he genuinely couldn't understand it. The hopes that had just built themselves back up again crumbled to dust in Julius's soul with such force he could almost hear them. Indignation and shame made his face blaze bright red.

"Wh-what, you got a problem with that?!"

And then something moved heavily on the other side of Harvey. The other side—outside the parapet. Julius opened his mouth in an "o" of shock, but he didn't manage to get any words out in time. Harvey seemed to get the picture from his expression anyway, because he immediately tried to dodge, but the swiping talons sent him flying backward, where he slid along the parapet.

One of *those monsters* sprang into view, leaping up and over the parapet from underneath the bridge, which it must have crawled up somehow without their noticing.

Unable to really respond right away, Julius only squeaked in surprise and backed up a few paces. Panic spread swiftly through the foot traffic on the bridge, too. He heard screams from every direction.

The thing's throat gurgled with something almost like a human moan as it came toward him on sticky, squelching feet. His gaze fixed on its pupil-less eyes, Julius couldn't force his trembling legs to run.

Squelch ... squelch.

The sound of its dragging footfalls echoing with strange clarity, it stuck out its tongue to lick a red hunk of flesh speared on its talons.

"Julius, get down!"

Before his body could respond to the voice, his heel slipped where he'd tried to step back, and he fell on his rear end. Something shot through the air above him just a hair's breadth from his head; and the monster, who'd been almost upon him, was knocked sideways by a blow to the temple. It got back up right away, though, without seeming to have taken much damage. One eyeball bulged out grotesquely from the impact, but it only tilted its head curiously, maybe not quite understanding what had happened, and then transferred its attention from Julius to the man who'd gotten in its way as it slowly stood up.

"Get back. You're in the way," Harvey said bluntly, and stepped in front of him. He held what looked like a steel pipe, which Julius guessed had come from the broken parapet. As he raised it, blood oozed out of a tear in the sleeve of his greatcoat. When he gritted his teeth hard and closed his eyes for just a second, a liquid like coal tar began to seep from the wound. His skin initially started to knit itself back together, but before long the liquid dried up and Julius could see him totter for a moment.

"A-ahh ... ah ..."

I have to help him. I have to do something.

Turmoil and fear still held his throat closed, and his brain hadn't thought any of it through clearly before his body charged forward.

With a loud yell, Julius full-body tackled the monster. He slammed it into the parapet, and he tried to keep going and push it right over, but its claws caught at his neck and almost brought him down with it. "Julius!" The shout was accompanied by a hand reaching out and grabbing his arm right in the nick of time. The monster plummeted down without him. Panting and clinging to the parapet with Harvey still gripping one arm, he looked down at the city below.

A shiver ran all the way down his spine.

The arched exits from the waterways that wove through every neighborhood in the city, dotting the towering inner walls partitioning it, were gaping open. And he could see droves of those greenish, drowned-corpse-like monsters crawling out of every one of them. A muddy green color overtook the inner walls as if foul water were oozing out. Julius stood riveted to the spot, staring at the horrific sight with the panic of the crowds running around on the bridge behind him for background music.

Then a ball of fire was launched into the flock of monsters crawling along the walls toward them. Julius couldn't tell from where. Watching them going up in flames and plummeting down from the walls filled him with even more nausea than relief.

He saw Security Forces soldiers with armor plating over their pure-white clerical robes appear in the town below. One platoon of them, brandishing their lit torches, came running up to the connecting bridge.

Julius recognized a familiar, heartening face at the lead.

"Dad!"

"Julius?! Are you all right?"

"What's going on—"

Julius's father noticed the lanky man with him and stopped in the act of leading his troops toward them. The two of them stared narrow-eyed at each other from a distance. It wasn't the time for a standoff, though; the monsters that had temporarily backed off under the torches' flames were already pressing close again. His father glanced over the parapet down to the land below and cursed softly. "They all came out of the sewer exits at once. They've shown up in the ordinary residential districts, too."

"What about Kieli? I heard she went to Lord Sigri's house—"

The words had hardly escaped his mouth before Harvey was suddenly climbing up onto the parapet and getting ready to jump down. "H-hang on a second! Don't jump from all the way up here!" Julius cried, panicked. He instinctively seized the collar of Harvey's greatcoat to stop him, which ended up more or less cutting off the man's airflow.

"Are you trying to kill me?!" Harvey bellowed, rubbing his neck with one foot still on the parapet.

"Hold on. The young lady isn't at Lord Sigri's. I got word that they'd run away," Julius's father explained calmly, taking hold of Harvey's arm.

"Run away?"

"We're guiding all the people in the residential districts to the cathedral. Try going there."

After he'd heard out Julius's father with narrowed eyes, Harvey nodded once and turned on his heel toward headquarters.

"Julius. You go, too."

"What about you?"

"This is my job."

Heart aching for his father staying behind to lead his men, Julius obeyed, wrenching himself away to take off running, too. As he made his way through the confusion, occasionally bumping into the people running this way and that, he called out to the tall form in priest's robes ahead of him. "Hey! Can Security Forces weapons take down monsters like that?"

"No," the man replied immediately, without even turning around. "The only way is to penetrate their hearts and break them. They're...my kind." His tone was emotionless, but he spat out that last part as if it tasted bad.

When they cleared the footbridge, the main gate into the Church headquarters' forest of steeples came into view. The front gate was jam-packed, overflowing with people fleeing town for the safety of the cathedral. They shoved each other, everybody trying to make it through first; old men fell to the ground amid the chaos; children sobbed as they were separated from their parents—

Unbidden, Julius's feet came to a stop. "...I'm going back. I should at least be able to help guide the evacuees."

Harvey turned to give him a dubious look. Julius met his eyes evenly and said in a strong voice, "You go look for Kieli. If you keep going straight ahead, you'll see the cathedral soon."

"...I don't need you to tell me that."

He was used to the needling by now and simply raised one hand in response before veering back in the direction they'd come from.

"Julius," said a voice behind him. He turned around to see that Harvey was still standing there looking at him. When

Julius paused for a moment and gave him a strange look, he went on rudely. "I think the way you seriously believe some-one like you can save the planet is so stupid it's funny."

"G-gee, excuse me! Don't call me back just to say that!" Julius shouted, his face beet-red with anger.

The other man abruptly smiled at him. "But…honestly, I also think you're amazing for being able to seriously believe it." The smile was softer than his usual smirk.

I didn't know he could smile this way…This unexpected side of Harvey plus the unexpected words made Julius fall silent in surprise.

"Hang in there!"

The man in priest's clothes took off with that cheer. Julius stood rooted to the spot for a while, watching him go until his coppery head disappeared into the chaos.

Hang in there—

For some reason, hearing those words from the man he'd always longed to catch up to made him want to cry. *You're the one who's so beaten up he can hardly walk, and you're cheering me on?*

"……You hang in there, too."

There was no way Harvey could still hear him. Still, Julius murmured the words and prayed that they'd be heard anyway. Then he spun around and took off running in the opposite direction.

From where she sat next to Kieli, Beatrix abruptly began darting her eyes all around them.

"What is it?" Kieli asked quizzically.

"...Mm, nothing. It's fine."

The woman who'd cut off the golden hair she was so proud of without a trace of regret smiled reassuringly at Kieli from beneath her black shawl. One section of that poor lopped-off hair was wrapped around Kieli's wrist as a good-luck charm. After they chatted awhile, a middle-aged woman sitting in front of them shot a glare. They exchanged looks and fell silent.

They both wore black clothes and black shawls. Pilgrims in dark-colored hats sat jostled up against each other in the pews packing the cathedral filled with gentle pipe organ background music. The great hall with its high vaulted ceiling was wreathed in a cool tranquillity at odds with the amount of people crammed into it. The faint scent of oil paintings wafting around them was the same one from Father Sigri's house. Had it worked its way into their clothes?

The pipe organ music ended, and a high-strung-looking old man dressed in long, pure-white robes trimmed in gold appeared on the balcony at the front wall. Though Kieli personally couldn't sense the slightest bit of godly power in him, reverent sighs escaped the congregation around her at the sight of him.

"I see that's not Father Sigri," Beatrix whispered, still staring forward. It was true; Father Sigri had stood at the platform for the worship service Kieli'd observed the other day, but today it looked like a different Elder would be giving the sermon. Straining her eyes, she made out Father Sigri waiting in the wings at the rear of the balcony, where he wouldn't be conspicuous. He had his right arm in a sling. *Oh, I get it. I guess*

he'd just unnecessarily upset the crowd if he stood on the plat-
form looking like that.

"Who'd have guessed you came from such a high-class family, huh?" Beatrix whispered half-teasingly. When Kieli frowned
in distaste, Beatrix shrugged a little and winked at her. "Hey,
it's a good thing, right? You found a parent."

Kieli shook her head back and forth. The fabric of her shawl
swung from side to side, slapping against her cheeks.

"You're not happy."

Kieli shook her head.

"Why not?"

"...Because the Church is the enemy for you and Harvey,"
she said darkly, looking down. Beatrix, on the other hand,
answered in a cheery, offhanded voice, "Eh, tiny issue."

"It's not tiny!"

Kieli's own voice rose before she knew it, and that same
middle-aged woman sitting in front of them glared again until
they exchanged another look and shrank back a little. Beatrix
lowered her tone to whisper, "Do you think Ephraim would
sweat a little detail like that?"

"Well...no..."

"Your happiness is always top priority. For him, and for me.
We're not worried about us, as long as *you* keep moving
forward. So...I'm sure lots more rough times are waiting
ahead, and it's okay if you run away or stand still sometimes,
but...never turn your eyes away from the future."

Her whisper next to Kieli's ear was soft, but so firm and
strong. With the left hand, the one wearing her good-luck
charm, Kieli grasped Beatrix's right hand where it lay next to

her on the pew and squeezed her beautiful fingers. "Stop it," she said in a scratchy whisper. "All of you—all of you stop saying things like that, like you're about to die. I don't want that. Don't leave me alone…"

Her own voice was weak and pitiful, but even so, what she said was her most heartfelt wish. Her prayer. She bit her lip against the threatening tears.

Beatrix's hand squeezed hers back firmly. Then she said in her usual utterly confident voice, "It's okay. You won't be alone. You'll get to see Ephraim."

"…Yeah. And you'll be with us forever, too, Beatrix." Forcing her tears back, Kieli squeezed her hand more tightly and nodded.

While they'd been concentrating on each other, a general stir had begun to ripple through the people around them. Even the middle-aged woman who'd glared at them whenever they talked was deep in conversation with the man next to her, frowning about something.

Beatrix and Kieli hadn't noticed it when everyone else had, since they hadn't been listening in the first place, but at some point the Elder's sermon had broken off. A wave of wariness swept over the congregation from the front of the room to the back.

What's going on…? Kieli straightened her back to sit up taller and peered through the heads of the crowd at the balcony. While the worshippers in their pews and the priests standing nearby all exchanged quizzical looks, the white-robed Elder on the balcony stood statue-still as though the sermon had completely vanished from his mind, staring pale-faced into the empty air.

For just an instant, Kieli saw a figure floating there above him. "Beatrix...!"

As she started and grabbed Beatrix's arm, a woman's shrill scream rose from somewhere in front of them.

Without warning, the Elder's body folded forward and pitched over the railing, plunging down from the balcony. Maybe to the congregation it looked as if he'd jumped—but Kieli had clearly seen an inky shadow grab the old man's robes and shove him. From where she sat, she couldn't see where he'd land, but she was pretty sure it was over ten meters from the balcony to the floor of the hall. There was an awful, heavy *thunk*. Screams rippled through the hall, and all the worshippers rose to their feet at once.

"Beatrix, did you see that? Just now—"

"I saw it. Don't get separated from me."

As the confusion swiftly engulfed the crowd, the two of them stood up, too, and pressed close to each other with their hands clasped tightly.

What happened? Why did he fall all of a sudden like that...?
Did he slip?
No, I saw it! I saw someone push him!

Unsettled whispers—it all overlapped perfectly in the back of Kieli's mind with the events from when she'd been a baby, the ones she'd seen in the paintings. She felt a vivid sense of déjà vu at the sight of the priests beginning to clear the bustling congregation from the room. This meant the next thing to happen would be—

Soon after the people started to follow the priests away, an enormous shadow fell over the electric lights illuminating the great hall.

Heh-heh-heh-heh-heh-heh!

Kyahahahahahaha!

Eerie animal laughs from all sides blended together and echoed off the arched ceiling. The torches adorning the walls crackled and shot out sparks, then exploded in a wave from the front of the hall to the back as if someone were raking the place with gunfire. All the lights were snuffed out, and the only illumination in the hall was the faint outside light from the stained-glass windows. Her vision hadn't adjusted to the dimness yet, but she could make out people screaming, people huddling together in fear, people curling themselves into little balls with their arms around their heads. With her hand in Beatrix's so they wouldn't get separated, Kieli was shoved by the confused crowd from all sides, jostled this way and that.

Then she spied a baby on the ground between the legs of the crowd, lost or left behind by its parents.

"Kieli—?!"

With a cry, she shook off Beatrix's hand and ran to the baby, snatching it up just before it could get stepped on and cradling it safely to her. "Are you okay?"

The instant Kieli peered into the face of the baby wrapped in its blanket, she gasped. The infant, not even a year old by Kieli's guess, came wide awake and fixed her with a murky, pupil-less gaze.

It twisted its mouth into an unpleasant grin.

Hyahahahahahaha!

The baby burst out laughing in a shrill, crazed voice, its plump young face filling with wrinkles before Kieli's eyes until it was old and shriveled. "No!" Kieli cried, and tried to let go, but the baby hung fast to her clothes with far too much strength for such tiny young hands; and no matter how hard she fought, she couldn't pull herself free. The baby's shrill laughter echoed on and on, out of place in the midst of the crowd's confusion.

She was stricken again by that vivid déjà vu.

The next thing to happen. The next thing to happen would be—

"That child did it! She's demon spawn!" someone yelled, pointing at them. The hysterical shouts wove their way through the crowd, spreading like wildfire among people who were already at the height of fear. They fell into a frenzy and mobbed Kieli, surrounding her and jostling as they tried to snatch the baby.

Her situation was the exact same as her mother Setsuri's had been back then.

The past was repeating itself. It was just like that day.

As Kieli's clothes and hair were pulled at from all directions, the creature in the blanket that had clung so hard to her and refused to let go abruptly vanished. The baby with the ancient face dissolved into a shadowy black mist, gliding smoothly up to the ceiling without a break in its crazed laughter. Looking up, Kieli's eyes met those of a narrow-faced man in glasses standing off to one side of the balcony, seemingly rooted to the spot, just looking on with a ghostly pallor—her father. Before she knew what she was doing, Kieli extended a pleading hand toward him through the crowd of people for help.

He took in her outstretched hand—and abruptly turned his gaze away, disappearing into the shadows of the balcony.

Some momentary half-formed hope broke inside her with an audible snap. The same despair her mother had felt flooded her heart.

Demon spawn! Demon spawn!

Kieli was the only one left penned in by the condemning crowd now, but their frenzy showed no signs of stopping. They kept on yelling and yelling as if possessed. The place felt almost like the exact opposite of a cathedral in the Church capital whose authority extended throughout the world; it could have been the gathering place of some violent heathen religion.

"Kieli! Kieli—"

She could hear Beatrix's faraway voice calling from across the throng of people, but she couldn't see her. Crazed faces surrounded her from all sides. Their railing was only a jarring sea of sound now, just violent percussion that held no meaning. *I'm scared...I'm scared...!* The fear robbed Kieli of the strength to resist them or shout anymore.

Help me, help me, HARVEY—!

When she finally couldn't help calling out for help to the man who wasn't here, she heard it:

"Stop it! Stop it!"

Someone was plowing his way through the crowd toward her, shouting. It wasn't Beatrix, and it wasn't Harvey either: It was the narrow-faced man in glasses, jet-black robes flapping as he ran through the crowd, elbowing the rioters violently aside to get to her and then immediately grabbing her arm.

"Stop it! I said let her go, you idiot!" the man shouted at one of the rioters who'd been pulling Kieli's hair and decked him.

One of the highest-ranking priests, someone who was supposed to be a man of character. Turned on a normal believer. Called him names. And hit him. With a closed fist.

In the center of the still-roaring chaos, Kieli gaped up at her father's desperate face as he crouched protectively over her, feeling almost like a bystander to some situation she had nothing to do with. The possessed expressions of the people pressing in on her and the commotion all around her—all the things she'd been so scared to death of a second ago—felt awfully distant and unreal. Her father was shouting abuse at them, but she couldn't really hear it. There was the warmth of her father's body as he held her. That was the only thing she could sense.

"Lord Sigri's taken leave of his senses!"

"Right now we need to take care of the late Father's body!"

She heard shouts, muted and far away.

Her father's voice shouting back, on the other hand, abruptly came through crystal-clear.

"Forget about a few senile old fools who were practically dead anyway and do some work!"

One of the highest-ranking priests, someone who was supposed to be a man of character. How could he say such a thing? Kieli couldn't believe her own ears.

"Why are there so many people here?!" Beatrix cried, irritably punching various people who blocked her path. She was sure there hadn't been so many people in the great hall during the service, but for some reason waves of them were pouring in from outside; by now they were all so tightly crowded together that they could hardly move. At this rate, she suspected they'd already crushed that Elder's fallen corpse underfoot.

"Kieli!" she shouted, casually hitting (with a closed fist) whatever random person happened to be getting in her way. Beatrix had seen her escape the hall with Father Sigri, so she did think the girl was probably okay for now, but still.

"Ah! I found you!"

That priest, Yoshiu or whatever his name was, forced his way through the crowd to her. He caught at her clothes as if to make sure she wouldn't get away from him again, his hand scrabbling somewhere around the waist of her dress.

"Watch where you're grabbing!"

"Huh? Oh! Ah—" The priest hurriedly let go of her, and then a confused look passed over his face as he wondered where he *should* grab. His hands sort of hung in the air as he thought. While he was thus preoccupied, a shove from behind sent him face-planting forward into her chest. "I-I'm so sorry!" he babbled, and immediately jerked away.

As he rubbed his bruised nose, he took a fresh look at her and blinked. "You've cut your hair straight!"

It's impossible to stay on guard around this guy... Beatrix sighed in disgust. "What's all this fuss about, anyway? Why are all these people coming here?"

"Oh, that's right! You see, something terrible has—"

A scream cut off the priest's explanation. It came from somewhere over the entrance—in no time, people were retreating from that direction, pushing their way back toward Beatrix. Across the wave of people, she saw a large greenish form. "Oh, no, they've made it here!" the priest shrieked pathetically, hiding behind her. In the center of the doughnut-shaped ring of people running around in panic, a single monster with skin gone mushy like a drowned corpse's ambled drunkenly forward.

...... So those are the Undying failures Kieli told me about.

"Well, this is just peachy," she complained to nobody in particular, and tested the weight of what she gripped underneath her shawl.

"L-let's run!"

Urged forward by the priest, who'd been more than ready to run from the beginning, Beatrix joined the tide of people fleeing from the monster for the time being. The crowd didn't seem to be running away from the monster attack so much as they were running to get ahead of everyone else. Screams rose up as people shoved each other aside or fell down. The cathedral that had been so wreathed in tranquillity a few short minutes ago was turning into a war zone, with all the ugliness of human nature on display and everyone acting as if the evil spirits had taken over their bodies.

And then the priest running in front of her gave a little cry and turned around, sort of hesitantly marching in place, so that Beatrix nearly crashed into him.

"What was that for?!" Beatrix started to complain, but he was already slipping past her and jogging a few meters back the way they'd just come. An old woman lay doubled over on the floor right in the middle of the brutal chaos; probably she'd fallen and hadn't been able to get up.

"Oh, dear Lord…dear Lord…" She was pressing her forehead to the floorboards, curled up around shaking clasped hands and muttering a string of prayers. Other people were stepping over her for the moment, but someone would step on her any second now.

"Grandma, what are you doing?! Get up!"

The priest embraced her and tried to help her stand. And that was when a great heavy shadow fell over their heads. With the old woman in his arms, the priest looked up and froze, all the blood draining from his face. The monster's claws came slashing down.

"Oh, for crying out loud!" Regripping the scissors underneath her shawl, Beatrix lunged without hesitation at the monster.

Clang!

She blocked its claws with the tip of the blades, then plunged them into one of the monster's eyes. If the thing really was an Undying, the blow wouldn't be even close to fatal, but it flinched back for a moment when she stole half its sight, and she took that opening to ram her shoulder into its torso with all her strength and send it flying. "Give me a break! I've only got this stupid thing for a weapon!" She kept on griping as she adjusted her hold on the scissors and squared off with the enemy she knew would probably be back on its feet any second.

She spared a glance at her own shoulder and clucked her tongue. Apparently she'd been clawed. There was a huge tear in her dress and a gaping wound on the exposed arm underneath. The monster's eyeball regenerated, and her own wound healed itself in parallel. Tumult swept over the people standing frozen around them.

"M-monster!" someone screamed. And who did they mean? Beatrix didn't even have to wonder. Obviously they wouldn't need to shout that about the thing that *looked* like a monster; they must be talking about *her*. Terror spread among them in the blink of an eye, and the petrified congregation started to run off in all directions again.

It was nothing new, but Beatrix couldn't stifle a frustrated grumble. *Boy, does it ever get on my nerves how everybody has to freak out and call me a monster over a little thing like this—*

"Um!" a timid voice suddenly spoke up from right nearby, as opposed to the retreating voices of all the other people scrambling to get away from her. The priest had secured the old woman and was peeking his ashen face out from behind the shelter of a pew back. At her sidelong glare of annoyance, he cringed a little as he asked her with hesitant concern, "Are… are you all right?"

Beatrix gaped at him with her mouth hanging open like a fool. The priest watched her face timidly, trying to gauge her mood.

She gave him a faint, wry smile.

"I'm fine. I almost wish it were stronger. You're in the way here, so hurry up and escape."

"Y-yes, ma'am!"

She watched the priest start moving deeper into the cathedral, helping the old woman along with him, out of the corner of her eye. Then she turned to face the monster again. The better part of the crowd had been retreating into the passageways at the rear of the cathedral, as if pressed back by the monster who'd appeared at the front door. Judging by the way the screams were growing fainter, the evacuation seemed to have mostly finished.

All right then, what to do now? Sure, she'd cracked a joke about wishing it were stronger, but if she were honest, she hadn't exactly thought much about how to compete with an enemy that had the same immortal qualities she did.

She glanced over its shoulder and let out a distinctly unrefined "Ugh..."

Several more monsters were shambling up the steps leading to the cathedral entrance with their swaying side-to-side gait. They distracted her for only a split second, but her opponent took advantage of it to launch itself at her in a bizarre leap she couldn't believe came from a bipedal walker. "Shit!" Beatrix seized one of the six-person pews and swung it with all her might into the monster. It hit dead center and broke apart. It seemed to only slow her enemy down; by the time the broken pieces of pew hit the floor, it was already right there in front of her. Out of its mouth, which gaped so wide she found herself wondering if its jaw was dislocated, peeked a rough tongue covered in viscous saliva and bumpy taste buds.

"Bea!" she heard a voice call. By that name she thought her family had called her a long, long time ago. By that insanely abbreviated nickname used by only one person left on this planet. At the same time, something skated along the floor toward her, spinning. Her reflexes knew what it was and had her ducking to pick it up before her brain even registered it.

A black big-bore gun with an ammo belt dangling from it. Wielding the bulky weapon in a two-handed grip, she leveled it at the enemy's heart.

Whump!

The thick gunshot sound unique to the carbonization gun rang out. The point-blank shot turned its whole chest to soot, leaving nothing but a gaping hole, and its nerveless body collapsed forward straight into her, pinning her to the ground beneath its heavyweight-class corpse. Beatrix screamed. The spongy feel of its skin, slack and moist just like a drowned man's, made her flesh crawl. "Gyah! No! Gross, get off me!" She thrashed her arms and legs like an overturned beetle until someone grabbed her arm with that same call of "Bea!" and managed to drag her out from under the slimy body.

When she turned around to look at it, half-crying where she sat on the ground clutching the man's arm, she saw its charred stone heart tumble out of the hole in its chest.

The corpse had returned to a mere corpse, never to move again.

"Phew…" When Beatrix heaved an undignified sigh, she felt one of her ribs twinge. *I guess that thing broke it in the fall…*

Ah, well, it was bound to heal up again before long. She just blocked out the pain and banished it from her thoughts to look at the guy who'd come to help her out.

They grinned at each other.

"Yo."

"Long time no see. You alive?"

They bumped fists. As two-year reunions between them went, that was about as emotional as it got. Beatrix's first impression was that on the one hand, he was disgustingly unchanged (well, not that she'd changed either), but on the other, he was now just about as far away from "whole and healthy" as you could get. The prosthetic hand she remembered from two years ago was gone, along with most of his right arm, and his left eye was a different color. Maybe he'd gotten another one.

He returned her slightly disgusted gaze with a gaze of his own and blinked.

"Something's different about you. Oh, you don't have enough hair!"

"I don't have *enough*? What kind of way is that to say it?!"

She decked him.

Then she shrugged and laughed softly, reaching out with that same hand to ruffle his copper-colored hair. "You're as beat-up-looking as always. It's very you."

"Qu-quit that!" The gruff way Ephraim tried to bat her hand away was so funny that she wanted to do it again.

"How're you doing, Pops?" she asked the radio dangling from Ephraim's neck, looking down, but the only answer from the speaker was a burst of static that seemed to object to the "Pops" thing. "Huh? Pops?" She looked back up at Ephraim.

"It broke, and it won't go back to normal…"

The way he lowered his eyes and bit his bottom lip despondently left her at a temporary loss for words, but she rallied. "Don't look so sad. It'll work out. You're the one who's always saying 'It'll probably work out somehow.'" Beatrix tugged on his bangs to drag his face up, then smiled at him. "It's a good thing you're here—hurry up and go find Kieli. I think she went around behind the cathedral. This thing still has bullets left, right? I'm borrowing it." Maybe he'd stolen it from a soldier he'd come across or something; the giant ammo belt unique to the carbonization gun still had plenty of rounds left in it.

"Bea?"

She stooped to pick up the carbonization gun. Ephraim caught her arm just as she finished standing back up. His copper eye peered at her worriedly. *He's onto me, eh?* With a self-deprecating smile, Beatrix put a hand to her side. The broken ribs were almost healed already.

"I'm fine. I've still got a little business to take care of, though. I'll catch up with you later."

While she'd been busy getting squashed by corpses and whatnot, she'd seen the newly arrived *failures* chase the pilgrims deeper into the building. In the same direction as that priest had taken off with the old lady. There was no going back now…Once you saved a guy the first time, you had to look after him till the end, or it left a bad taste in your mouth like nobody's business.

"Beatrix," she heard him call one more time just as she was about to run off with the carbonization gun slung over one shoulder. "Mm. What?" she said, stopping. She kept her tone

casual, but she knew perfectly well that when he called her by her actual full name, he was trying to say something serious.

There was a pause before his next line came.

"...Let's all go home together," he said, staring at the ground as if he was embarrassed and glowering shyly. Beatrix blinked stupidly at him for a moment, then gave a suppressed laugh.

He might seem as though he hadn't changed underneath all those new scars, but it really hit her now how somewhere along the line, he had. *He never used to show his feelings so openly on his face like this before.* It had been only a few short years in a life almost a century long. And yet for them those few short years had brought new meetings substantial enough to effect at least a bit of change in what had dragged on and on unchanging for so long before.

"Well, duh. I'll catch up with you soon." She reached up with one hand and dragged the coppery head even higher than her own into a light embrace and said, "You do your best on your own, too."

The same thing she'd said to her baby brother a long, long time ago.

This time, she managed to make that line—the one she'd spat coldly as a young girl who couldn't express her feelings right—come out soft and warm.

Only a few short years, during which she'd undeniably changed, too. She didn't regret them at all.

With that promise to meet again, the two of them each took off running in different directions.

*　　　*　　　*

Why aren't any Church Soldiers coming?

Isn't it the Security Forces' job to protect the people at times like these?

Oh, dear Lord…

The pile of pews they were using to barricade the door to the supply room they'd fled into gave a weird, squealing clatter. There was only one monster on the other side. Nonetheless, even with the combined strength of all the men pushing it back, the barricade creaked away as if it was ready to break at any second. They had a few young priests there in addition to the pilgrims; as Yoshiu joined them in bracing the barricade, he listened with half an ear to the whining and complaining gradually starting up among the women and children and elderly huddled together in the back of the supply room watching them.

The Security Forces are probably doing everything they can, too. Far more packs of monsters were showing up in the city streets, and if this was what *one* of them was like, he doubted Security Forces equipment would be enough to easily hold them all off. And yet only a handful of them had made it all the way up to the Church building—these people who couldn't come up with anything to do but complain at a time like this probably didn't give a thought to the fact that it was the Security Forces' hard work they had to thank for that. Still, he had no right to criticize anyone. He felt like airing a complaint or two himself.

Whether he'd let his muscles slacken as he thought or it had just broken through, the monster's arm abruptly thrust through a gap between the legs of two pews, ripping a scream from the priest's throat.

Bony fingers with slack greenish skin and sharp claws squirmed like an insect's writhing limbs, trying to grab its prey through the barricade. The men at the barricade screamed in terror, and so did the people behind them. "Nngah!" The arm reached out and seized a young man right next to Yoshiu by the neck. His madly struggling body was yanked flush against the barricade from the other side; Yoshiu pulled it back with every ounce of his might from this side. Just when he and two other priests had managed to wrestle the man away from it, the monster's arm snapped in half at the elbow with an eerie *crunch* that gave him goose bumps. Everyone around screamed and jumped away from where it had landed on the floor.

The creepy wrenched-off forearm kept squirming, crawling along the floor with just its fingernails as if it were still searching for prey even now. They all gave it a wide berth, staring at it pale-faced. He heard a child's shrill voice start to cry. The barricade started to creak again, and everyone desperately formed a wall to hold it up.

"Help me! Please!" called a human voice unexpectedly from the other side. When Yoshiu pressed his face up to the crack between the pews and peered out, he saw a man who seemed to have fallen behind the rest standing there pleading. A pilgrim, he thought. The now one-armed monster noticed this new arrival and sluggishly turned its gaze to focus on him.

"Help me, let me in, please! Now!"

Some of the men slackened their hold on the barricade at his panicked begging, but then one of the onlookers behind them protested, "Don't!"

"Don't open it, or that thing will get in, too!"

Yoshiu couldn't believe his ears. A normal civilian who hadn't run as quickly as they had was outside, and this woman was telling them not to open the barricade. And even more unbelievably, a chorus of others cried out in agreement. "Sh-she's right. Don't do it!" "We've got no choice. He was just unlucky." "But…." There were a few people who looked as if they wanted to object, but they were cowed into silence by the majority.

"What are you waiting for?! Please, hurry up and open it! Help me!"

They could still hear a man's voice pleading for help from beyond the creaking barricade, but the people on the inside only exchanged dark looks. In the end, there wasn't a single person who tried to relax the barricade. The man screamed on the outside, and everyone inside flinched. His voice, still screaming "Help me, help me," grew steadily thinner and fainter.

As he held up the barricade with everyone else, thoughts swirled in Yoshiu's mind. *What should I do? I have to help him. But that monster really will come in here the moment we let down the barricade. What should I do? What should I do—? Why won't God reach out a hand to save us at a time like this? Is even* this *a trial?*

"You! Out of the way!"

Out of nowhere, a sharp voice calling from outside. "You" wasn't nearly specific enough to actually get anything done, though; they were all too flabbergasted to move, let alone get out of anyone's way, when—

Whump!

A dull explosion like a blast of compressed air rang out on

the other side of the barricade. One section of it collapsed with a clatter; a split second after the men nearby leapt aside, screaming, the greenish monster fell through along with a broken pew. Screams sounded around him, and the crowd backed up all the way to the rear wall.

There was a beat of questioning silence. But the monster stayed slumped facedown over the pew, with no sign of movement.

Just as the mood of the crowd was beginning to turn from fear to puzzlement, a figure leapt up and over the barricade from the other side, using the monster's back as a springboard and landing on the floor with a loud bang. A stir swept through them as they looked up. The sight of her, her shortened golden hair floating up around her and scattering reflected light all around as she flew through the air as if on golden wings, was just like—

Just like—

"An angel," he heard someone murmur with a sigh.

She flew nimbly, gorgeously as an angel through the air and alighted on the floor without even a wobble. The next moment, though, the people's reverent sighs were replaced by a stir of repulsion. They took in the sight of her properly, carrying a blood-covered man who must've been bitten by the monster slung over one shoulder and a black big-bore gun braced against the other.

"Monster…" he heard the ones who'd seen her abnormal healing powers whispering to each other.

Meanwhile, she just dumped the injured man rather roughly on the ground without appearing to pay any attention to their terror and said flatly, "Do you have a doctor or anything in here?" She scanned the faces of the crowd. "If somebody doesn't patch him up quick, he's done for." The priests there who knew first aid rushed, if timidly, to help him.

"Only one of them here? There were more, weren't there?" the woman quizzed them further, gesturing with a wave of one hand at the monster, which showed no signs now of ever moving again. Yet nobody in the crowd moved to answer her question. Impulsively, Yoshiu cried out, "There were some people who ran into the other passageway! I think the others probably followed them…" When her crystal-clear, ice-blue eyes fixed on him, they stole his breath, and he closed his mouth.

And then she flashed him a first-class smile that shot straight through the hearts of everyone who saw it, just as it always did.

"Okay. Thanks."

She spared only a brief glance at the people still keeping their distance and looking on with those repulsed gazes before she spun around and flew back through the barricade, once again using the monster's corpse as a springboard. Apart from the priests tending to the wounded man, the crowd around him just watched her go without reacting.

"…Ah!" Yoshiu, who'd been just watching her go right along with them, jolted back to himself and elbowed his way through them, diving into the hole she'd left in the barricade. He hesitated to touch the monster's body, but then he averted his eyes and crawled up over it anyway (the spongy feel of it, its sort of foul, bloody stench, and the burnt smell mixed in with it all made his stomach roil and his eyes burn with tears) to get to the other side. When he landed in the corridor outside the supply room, he cried, "W-wait, please!"

At his call, the woman running down the passage with a carbonization gun on one shoulder stopped and turned to him.

"What? It's dangerous here, so go back and fortify the barricade or something."

"I—well—that is—" Yoshiu stopped a little ways from her, his tongue suddenly faltering.

She blinked curiously at him a couple of times and then went, "Oh," as if she suddenly understood, although he hadn't actually said anything yet. "Right, I guess you need to capture me, don't you?"

"No, that's not it," he denied anxiously, shaking his head… *You don't really have to go help them, do you? You should just leave those ungrateful wretches to their fate.* That's what he'd dashed out here to tell her. But now that it was time to actually form the words, he hesitated. It was just such an awfully selfish thing to say right after she'd saved *him*. It disgusted him how cowardly and narrow-minded he was. *There's something wrong with this—did I really pass the priesthood exam?* The idea was starting to seem incredible.

"The one I need to capture is the weapon of massacre and the 'Demon of War' and the 'Witch of Toulouse,'" he said, thinking hard about each word. "Not you."

She looked mystified. He himself didn't really know what he'd been trying to say, for all the thought he'd put into it. He bit his lip, impatient with himself for not being able to put what he wanted to say into words.

"When we first found you, the town kids were all excited, calling you an angel, and to be honest I thought it was ridiculous…but…" He took a breath, and then after a moment continued. "But the woman who arrived at my place out of nowhere that day really was an angel…"

After the words were out of his mouth, he realized he might have just babbled something horribly cheesy. Fierce embarrassment seized him. He couldn't bear to look into her astonished face, so he looked down, cheeks flaring. *Wh-what the heck am I saying?! That almost sounded like a love confession!*

But staring at the floor in silence soon became unbearable, too, and before long he risked a glance up through his bangs to check her expression.

"……Thanks!"

She smiled—smiled that exquisite first-class smile just for him—and then sprinted off into the chaos where the monsters still roamed.

✿

"Out of bullets, huh…"

The ammo belt was empty. She let the carbonization gun fall to the floor with a heavy thud. She was in a pillar-lined passageway toward the rear of the cathedral. At her feet, where gunpowder smoke was currently settling, lay the bodies of the *failures* she'd shot through the heart. They weren't exactly giving the place a pleasant atmosphere. She'd used up her weapon, but she was pretty sure she'd taken out all the ones who'd gotten into the cathedral now. Maybe there were a few more who'd made it into the headquarters facilities farther into the Church complex, but if that meant they were attacking the Elders and high-ranking priests who'd hightailed it out of here without a thought for anybody else, Beatrix sure wasn't going to waste any pity on them.

Blowing out a deep breath, she sat down with her back propped against a pillar to take a little break.

"Sheesh..."

She grumbled in annoyance at the tears all over her clothes. This had been the simple black dress she'd liked the best out of all the ones that had been bought for her while she was imprisoned (ensconced) in the Sigri residence. Beatrix's body was pretty tattered, too, what with little cuts and big cuts and bruises and all, but unlike the dress, her body was salvageable, so she wasn't bothered about that (maybe normal people would prioritize things in the other order).

She let her gaze drift casually over the bodies strewn at her feet.

"You were victims, too, weren't you? I'd like to give you a funeral service, but that's not in my job description, you know? And this place is crawling with priests, after all."

She wondered if Ephraim had gotten to see Kieli yet. A wry laugh escaped her with the sigh. That boy just took so much looking after. Even an angel wouldn't go this far looking after a stranger!

An angel, hmm...?

Remembering the priest's words to her, she felt just the teensiest bit flattered. One minute she was being called a witch in Toulouse, and the next thing she knew somebody was saying she was an angel. Frankly, she preferred "witch." It was a lot less work than being an angel.

I mean, angels have to do "good things" for people.

Then again, for today at least she thought she'd made a damn fine angel, if she did say so herself.

In between two pillars she saw a large painting. The portrait of a flock of angels ascending to Heaven surrounded by saints was blurred with the smoke drifting along the floor of the passageway.

Thank you! It's wonderful! It's wonderful! she heard a sunny voice say from within it. In the yard of the tidy white house, a golden-haired girl in a brand-new white dress laughed merrily as she danced around and around and around. A little boy chased his sister around as she ran until he tripped and fell flat on his face. *Sheesh, don't you know boys don't cry?* the girl lectured him when he looked ready to cry over his scraped knees, lifting him to his feet.

You do your best on your own, too—why had she said the same words to Ephraim then that she'd said to her little brother at their parents' funeral? Ephraim never stopped needing looking after, and deep down he was a scaredy-cat who couldn't make up his mind about anything, and he was way too fast to get tears in his eyes for somebody that pig-headed...Yeah, now that she thought about it, she guessed he must've been pretty much just like a little brother to her this whole time.

Let's all go home together.

Ephraim's final words floated through her mind. Right, she couldn't afford to be taking a break yet; she needed to get moving. So they could all go home together.

"Okay, gotta go. I'd better do a little more babysitting."

She tried to stand up, but her still-tired legs lurched a little. "Get your act together," she snapped at them, putting a hand against the pillar to steady herself.

And then, out of the corner of her eye, she saw the monster corpse lying by the next pillar over slide a few centimeters. Beatrix's eyes widened in disbelief. *I shot that thing through the heart! How can it still move?!* It crawled along the floor still facedown and disappeared beyond the pillar.

Strange things that looked like broken-off cables were dragged along with it into the shadows. And then she began to hear the crunching of teeth on flesh and bone.

"....?"

When she stared quizzically in that direction—

Shunk.

Beatrix felt a baffling pressure as though something were bearing down on her heart from above. When she tried to stand up, she crashed back down onto her rear end, unable to support her own weight.

She saw a giant misshapen form on the other side of the pillar. Dragging all manner of fat and thin cables and pipes of all sizes from various parts of its body like a scrapped machine, it lurched heavily out of the pillar's shadow.

Still sitting flat on the floor, Beatrix widened her eyes in horror. She couldn't believe what they were telling her. Her voice trembled.

"You're..."

❧

The sensation of her father's left hand pulling at her own right hand was frying Kieli's brain. It didn't feel like Harvey's hand or Beatrix's hand or her grandmother's hand. She couldn't find the words to describe it, couldn't process it in her mind. Her thoughts were all mixed up. *I don't get it. I don't get it. I don't get it...*

"P-please let me go," she said weakly, finally finding the voice to refuse.

"A-ah, right. I'm sorry." Her father let go of her hand apologetically. They were both breathing pretty hard. They stopped running and just walked briskly for a while in silence. Her father's glasses were gone, and a bruise was forming to one side of his mouth. She wondered if he'd taken a punch from someone in that frenzied chaos in the cathedral.

...Because he'd helped Kieli.

They'd managed to escape the chaos, and now they were walking along the colonnade connecting one of the headquarters buildings to another tower. Thin beams of outside light filtered in from between the thick columns; the space stretching out in a long line before them was wreathed in a dusky tranquility very like the one she'd felt in the cathedral before. The distant commotion they'd been able to hear from that cathedral most of the way here had faded out of earshot behind them at some point. Their two sets of footsteps and still-irregular breaths echoed in the deserted colonnade.

"Are you hurt...?" her father asked tentatively, and Kieli firmly shook her head. His bruised face broke into a smile, as if this relieved him. Even though he was the one who'd been punched, who was enduring a black eye, and he'd lost the sling for his right arm at some point, too, so that his arm hung painfully and unnaturally from his shoulder. The conversation petered out after that, and uncomfortable silence reigned again for a while.

Kieli abruptly came to a stop, so her father stopped, too, looking at her as if he was wondering what was wrong.

"This—this isn't—" She looked down at the tips of her boots as she spat the words out, scooting backward a little to get away from him. "This isn't—wh-why are you...? You'd better not think this is enough to win me over!" She knew as she spoke that she was blurting out horrible things, but her head was all messed up and she didn't know what she should say. She wished somebody would come rescue her that very moment. *No, I don't want to be left alone with him. Harvey, Corporal, Beatrix...!* The anguished expression on his face, lips pressed tightly together, made the atmosphere between them even more unbearable.

"I...I have to go back to Beatrix."

"Wait—"

She shook off her father's hand when he reached out to stop her and took off in the direction they'd come.

This time Kieli really was at her limit. She didn't know what she might do if she stayed with him any longer. She was sure to blurt out something that would make Harvey look sad again. She'd hated herself more and more each day she'd been here.

Your happiness is always top priority—

Beatrix had said that, said it about *her* as though she deserved it somehow, and how could she face the people who felt that way about her if she kept doing this?

Kieli heard a low, animal gurgle from somewhere nearby.

She came to a halt, chilled to the bone. She could see a large human form in the shadow of one of the colonnade's pillars.

Posture stooped like an animal's, swaying from side to side, it tilted its head and gurgled again inquisitively as if it was making sure it knew what she was. A *failure*—

Kieli's father stepped in front of her where she'd frozen in place mid-run. Still, the arm he'd thrust out to protect her with was quivering slightly. The *failure* took a step out from behind the pillar, and Kieli's stiff feet moved jerkily backward at her father's push.

After that one step, though, the failure abruptly folded forward and collapsed facedown on the floor. Kieli's eyes widened incredulously—it was just so sudden—and then she turned them away instinctively a moment later, swallowing back the rising nausea.

Half the fallen failure's body was missing, as if it had been bitten off.

"This tastes nasty," she heard a different voice say in the shadows. There, holding a bloody stone heart in his right hand and noisily slurping up the blood and meat sticking to the end of a bio-cable dangling from the corner of his mouth—someone Kieli knew—

Horrified, Kieli made her lips form his name. "Joa…chim…?"

"Sheesh," the lean man in black robes muttered in an incongruously breezy voice, sighing and shrugging. "You said you couldn't ever get it back, but that was a lie, wasn't it, Pops? Or else what are you hiding behind your back?" Kieli shrank back in surprise when he fixed her with a look over her father's shoulder. Her father took a step forward protectively.

"*You* got something back, didn't you…What a liar."

And out of the shadow of the pillar walked Joachim, with

the same sluggish steps those monsters had. Kieli sucked in a startled breath when she saw how strange his appearance had become. Half the left side of his body, which he'd been hiding behind the pillar, had turned to a mass of rotting green flesh, and globs of rotten meat dribbled down from the fingertips of the left hand he dangled lifelessly at his side. As he nibbled at the stone heart in his right hand just as though he were sipping sweet fruit nectar, he gave a strange, hiccupping laugh.

"Say, I wonder which of you it would be more fun to hurt by killing the other one," he said, facing them and cocking his head curiously.

"Run," whispered her father, shoving Kieli back. She let him, and began to tear off down the passage, but before long she tripped over her own fear-stiffened feet. Her father caught her before she fell and tugged her hand; they began running together.

A steel door was visible at the end of the dusky colonnade ahead. She could sense leisurely steps following them from behind. They made it to the other side, checking over their shoulders all the way, and her father seized the doorknob and pushed. This entrance evidently wasn't used very often; the door was thick with rust, and all it did was creak under his hands. Unable to bear to watch any longer, Kieli stood next to her father and rammed her body into the rusty door with all the strength she could muster. Their only warning was a squeal of metal before it flew open with surprising force, and their momentum sent them half-falling through it to the other side.

The darkness was deeper here than it had been in the colonnade outside, and the air was thick with rust and dust and a foul odor. They were in a sort of cylindrical tower. When Kieli looked up, she saw walls crawling with fine cracks and a spiral staircase running along them and disappearing into the darkness above.

A low groaning sound like wind blowing down from above echoed dully against the walls.

While they'd struggled with the door, the presence pursuing them had gotten much closer. Kieli was already panting, but her father dragged her forward by the hand and they ran up the narrow staircase that would allow only one fully grown adult to pass at a time. She could hear two sets of footsteps jogging up the concrete steps... And the thwacking of a third set of footsteps coming leisurely after them from behind. He was walking slowly, and yet the impression that he was steadily closing the distance between them set her nerves on edge.

Kieli wasn't sure how high they'd climbed, but her already leaden feet stumbled and missed the next step, and she tumbled forward and whacked her shin. She knocked her father off balance in front of her, too, through their joined hands. He managed to regain his balance, though, and lent Kieli a hand to help her up. But while they'd paused, the footsteps approaching from behind had grown quite close.

In the dim stairway they had only a few meters' visibility. A tall man appeared out of the darkness below.

The arm he slashed out sent her father flying. The priest's back slammed into the wall, and he slumped down onto the steps. With a little scream, Kieli immediately tried to run to him, but an arm hooked around her neck from behind and ripped her away. Her father only lay there on the floor, groaning, and didn't get up. He had a hand to one shoulder. Had he hit the one that had been dislocated?

"Let me go!"

As she struggled, the hand around her neck grabbed her jaw and squeezed. The skin of his palm was squishy; the feel of it pressing into her jaw sent a thrill of horror down her spine. He pressed her back against the railing of the spiral staircase until she was half bent backward over it. Directly below her head was a column of fathomless darkness.

"Stop…it…" she heard her father grunt. Joachim tossed a glance over his shoulder without releasing Kieli and clucked his tongue. "To hell with you. *You* have something you're desperate to protect, don't you? You got something, didn't you? That pisses me off. You traitor," he spat as he wrapped his hands around Kieli's throat and began to choke her. "Ngh…" Kieli desperately tried to force her own hands between Joachim's to buy herself an airway. Her vision flickered with the lack of oxygen.

As she writhed in pain, Joachim drew his face in close to hers and licked his lips in anticipation. The stench of death assailed her nose.

"Are—humans tasty…? That meat—before tasted—nasty…"

His grip loosened by a fraction, letting air back into Kieli's lungs.

"Jo…a…?" she gasped out brokenly, trying her best to call his name through her fit of coughing. She thought he was acting weird. His eyes that had been the same pretty blue-gray as the night sky were clouded with white now, and they weren't both focusing on the same point. "Joachim…Joachim!" she called to him, still coughing; his blue-gray eyes bulged and rolled around in his head just millimeters away from her face until they finally focused, and then he looked at her.

"Ki—eli…help me…" he said in a hiccupping voice, his cheeks distorted into a bizarre, sad, pained smile. "It's weird—my whole body keeps hurting—but I can't shut out the pain… I can't remember how…I can't think—I can't *think*. Hey, is there anything weird about me right now?"

"Joachim…!"

"Hey, do me a favor, Kieli."

Pushing her into the railing with one hand wrapped around her neck, Joachim used his half-rotten other hand to take Kieli's and press it to his own chest. His eyes rolled and bulged again, and then he turned his gaze to her with a sad expression.

"Dig my heart out," he implored her. Kieli widened her eyes in terror. "Dig it out for me, come on…Help—me, let me rest…"

"No! No! I can't! Let me go!" As she struggled to get free, Kieli shook her head as hard as she could in refusal. Her hand sank effortlessly into his chest, which almost seemed to swallow it up. With a ragged scream, she tried to pull it back out.

Traitor…

In her dimming consciousness, she heard him curse her not with her ears, but echoing deep inside her skull.

Bits of conversations she'd had with Joachim since they'd

gotten to the capital floated into her mind and then disappeared again like bubbles.

I'm going to kill your dad, you know.
Whatcha crying about?
You and I are birds of a feather.
So you know what? I'll give you a hand with this. I'll kill your enemy for you.
You're nothing like me after all.

Traitor—had she betrayed him? First she'd said she didn't mind if he killed her father—she'd said her father was an enemy—and then when push came to shove she'd hesitated, and she'd tried to stop him in the end. She'd gotten all confused hearing her father's words and feeling his warmth, and she'd been rejecting him as hard as she could, desperate not to be won over. Just now, when her father had been knocked down, she'd immediately tried to run to him. Was acceptance a betrayal? She didn't know. She didn't know what to do. *Somebody help me—*

"Joachim!"

It was like being shaken awake from a nightmare: the voice in her dimming ears abruptly snapped her mind back into focus.

Joachim stopped moving. With her back shoved up against the railing and her neck bent backward, Kieli swept her gaze over everything she could see of the tower. A tall, lean figure ran up out of the darkness that sank over the bottom of the staircase. In those jet-black robes that melted into the dark, for a moment she almost mistook him for someone else, but there was no mistaking that dull gleam of red hair in the gloom, or the voice that reached Kieli's ears loud and clear without his having to raise it. No mistaking it. Even though she was still being held captive, an inexpressible feeling of relief spread within her heart.

The new arrival stopped a little ways below them on the steps, panting.

"Yo. The hero's showing up at the perfect time," Joachim said teasingly, holding him in check by clenching a hand around Kieli's chin.

Grinding his teeth and aborting the step he'd been about to take, Harvey shouted, "What the hell are you doing, Joachim?!"

"What does it look like I'm doing? I'm in the middle of a murder-suicide with your precious Kieli, obviously."

Joachim forced her even harder against the railing, until her upper body doubled over backward and began to slide down. Her entire field of vision was a darkness that stretched endlessly down, down, down, framed by black bubbles popping at the edges as her head swam. Joachim and Harvey glared at each other from their respective high and low positions.

While they were distracted by the staring contest, Kieli sensed something moving behind Joachim.

"Let go of my daughter!"

Sigri pounced at Joachim from behind in a sort of tackle. Joachim seemed slightly surprised, but he shoved the Elder off with a jab of one elbow and then knocked him over with a merciless karate chop to his right shoulder. Sigri sank back to the floor by the wall again. But Kieli, who'd been released from Joachim's arms in the meantime, had already slid to the ground and half-rolled down the stairs away from him.

Harvey's priest's-cloth-covered legs appeared before her eyes as he stepped protectively in front of her.

Cursing, Joachim rubbed some rotting flesh off his chin. Then he turned and sprinted unsteadily up into the towering wall of darkness that shrouded the top of the spiral staircase. For a moment Harvey moved to follow him, running two or three steps up, but he stopped almost right away. The sound of retreating footsteps was swallowed up by the darkness overhead. Holding a hand to her throat and gasping, Kieli looked up to where the sound of his footsteps was fading into the distance. He'd already vanished from sight.

Sigri was lying midway up the stairs. Harvey stooped a little to check on him and then returned to the step where Kieli sat.

Kieli still coughing a little, Harvey still panting slightly— their eyes met.

The tall form squatting in front of her pulled her gently into a hug.

Kieli bit her trembling lip and tried desperately to hold back her tears, but once one of them managed to spill out in a single fat drop, there was no stopping them anymore. "Aaaa… Aaaaaaa, Harvey…!" She wound her jelly-limp arms around his back as tightly as she could and buried her face in his chest while she gasped for breath. Tearfully, she called his name over and over again. "Harvey, Harvey, Harvey." Over and over and over again.

Each time, she heard him whisper "Yeah" into her ear. The

familiar comfortable voice and the familiar tobacco smell. "Sorry I'm late."

She shook her head from side to side without lifting it from his chest. He'd come for her. He'd come for her just as he'd promised. He'd said he'd come no matter what, so he'd come when she was in trouble. That was enough for Kieli.

"What about Beatrix?"

"I saw her. It's okay now. We can go home together soon."

She soaked up the quiet, comforting voice all the way down to the bottom of her heart, and the tears just kept coming. She'd just finished shaking her head, and now she was nodding over and over. *We can go home soon. We can go home together.* How long had she waited to hear those words these past few days? Each one had felt like a month.

Clang.

The sound of a door creaking shut far above them. With a groan, cool outside air flowed into the musty inside wind that had been echoing bitterly off the walls. Harvey looked up once, then drew away a little from Kieli.

"Can you wait for a few minutes? I want to have a talk with that idiot. I'll be back soon, okay?"

Kieli made an uneasy face, but nonetheless she swallowed back the urge to stop him. She gave a tiny nod. She was sure this was another thing Harvey needed to settle for himself so they could all go home together...and if that's how it was, Kieli couldn't stop him.

It was so they could all go home.

Harvey nodded back at her reassuringly. He lifted the radio from his neck and handed it to her, then stood up and took off up the stairs. Hugging the radio to her, Kieli watched him go until his priest's robes vanished into the darkness. The radio began to croon a quiet, lullaby-like static for the unease deep in her heart that she still couldn't quite banish.

"Corporal..." When she pressed her forehead to the speaker, she caught the faint sound of the radio's voice through the static.

Kieli crawled just one step closer to where Sigri lay and tried to assess how he was. He didn't move. Was he unconscious? She closed the distance only that little bit, though; she couldn't go any closer, and she couldn't speak either, so she just curled herself into a ball a little ways away from her father, hugging the radio and feeling uncomfortable.

There were still things weighing on Kieli's mind that needed to be settled for them to go home together. Things that Kieli had to settle by herself—Kieli, and no one else.

He took the stairs all the way up to the top. Once he'd cleared them in one long dash, he stopped and exhaled, then took just a few more deep breaths to get his lungs under control.

Chilly outside air blew in through the half-open steel door in front of him. As soon as he stepped through it and came out into the open air, a strong mountain wind hit him hard enough to almost knock him over before he managed to grab the door frame. A long, open cloister stretched out in front of him toward a neighboring tower. He had the rock faces of the mountain range to one side of him, and to the other side he had one of the city's sheer inner walls plummeting straight down into the distance. Far below him, Harvey could see the "mechanical city" enveloped in gray smog and the overpasses of the railroad that cut through it.

And then he saw one knee crumple underneath Joachim and send him falling right about halfway through the cloister. The wind was blowing hard and Harvey was still breathing fast, but he closed the distance between them at a dead sprint. Joachim turned and jabbed a folding knife at him as soon as he'd picked himself up from the floor. Harvey parried it, though he did take a shallow cut to the back of his hand in the process, and grabbed his opponent's arm. They both tumbled over and rolled along the floor of the cloister as they wrestled for control of the knife. When they came to a stop, Harvey was straddling Joachim, the tip of Joachim's knife was pressed to his jugular, and Harvey's hand was gripping the dead center of Joachim's chest, right above his heart. They glared at each other in that position, where with the next moment's movement either of them could put the other out of commission, at least temporarily.

The decay was progressing. Harvey could see the skin of Joachim's cheek crumbling horribly right before eyes as the other man stretched it into a smile and gave a bizarre *hee-ha* laugh.

"Did you come to laugh at me? You came to laugh and call me pathetic, didn't you?"

"I'm not gonna laugh."

"So, what, are you gonna be nice and kill me, then?"

"Yeah. It'll be my pleasure."

Harvey channeled more force into the hand gripping his

opponent's chest. He felt the sensation of his fingers sinking into putrefied skin. However, he stopped moving there.

"What's the matter? Do it. Or else *your* head's gonna roll."

He flexed his hand and a thin line of blood welled up under the tip of the blade at Harvey's throat, but Harvey still didn't push him any harder. Joachim twisted the corners of his mouth up in a smile. "What's that look for? What, are you pitying me *now*? You know this was all your fault in the first place. You piss me off. You seriously piss me off full tilt, heart and soul, you know that?!" The last few words came out like a war cry as he flipped them over so that he was on top. They rolled together a few times until Joachim's back hit the railing.

Apparently it had grown brittle. A whole section of the stone rail gave way in a clatter of falling rock that kicked up clouds of mineral dust everywhere. Joachim fell backward right along with it.

Quicker than thought, Harvey found himself bending his upper body over the edge of the cloister and grabbing Joachim's wrist in the nick of time. His shoulder creaked under the burden of a grown man's full weight. At the same time, a sickening sound like some viscous substance tearing apart met his ears. Joachim's half-decayed left arm ripped at the elbow joint, until he dangled only by a few last threads of tendon or nerve fiber or something.

Below the cloister plummeted the sheer inner walls of the city, oozing dirty sewer water from every crevice. Far beneath them he could see an angular rocky slope. Harvey wasn't sure even an Undying could come back to life if he fell headfirst from this height and dashed his brains out, and he'd never tested it, either.

Hanging by one arm over a drop of something like forty meters, Joachim arranged his face into a taut, mocking smile as if the whole thing had nothing to do with him.

"You know, I don't get you at all. You make no damn sense. Why'd you save me after that whole speech about killing me?"

"You're the one who makes no damn sense!" Harvey bellowed back as he supported Joachim's weight with every ounce of his strength.

"What were you trying to accomplish? What did you *want*?! First you hang around me, getting in my way all the time, and then you ask me to kill you? What the hell is that?! What the hell did you want from me?!"

The words were coming out of his mouth without passing through his brain first. He hadn't particularly intended to give this guy a lecture like this. Why was he getting so worked up over a guy like this?

Harvey could feel certain that he was glad he'd taken the path he had, that he had no regrets. But this guy—had anything ever satisfied him a little? Had there ever been anything he could feel glad for? He always resented every stupid little thing; he always looked like he hated everything; what had he, himself, wanted all this time—? It wasn't that Harvey pitied him or wanted to save him or whatever. He was just venting his irritation at not being able to *understand*. Sometimes their paths had crisscrossed and sometimes they'd run parallel to each other, but all the same, he felt as if he'd always been walking the same distance as Joachim. If he'd traveled just a slightly different path, maybe he would have ended up just like this guy. This guy was another him who'd traveled a different path. A him who hadn't been able to find anything.

The mocking little smile vanished from Joachim's face. He looked straight up at Harvey with those sickeningly familiar blue-gray eyes. Their gazes met for a moment.

And then Joachim said with a sigh, "You just never stop being a sickeningly softhearted moron, do you? That's why I hate your stupid ass. What was I trying to do? What did I want?......No way am I telling *you* that. Moron."

The same old familiar invective, and then—

With the folding knife in his right hand, he cut the tendon at his left elbow that was the last thing supporting his own weight.

"Joachim!"

Falling headfirst with his left forearm still in Harvey's hand, Joachim smirked and pointed his right thumb to his chest. Then he plunged the folding knife into it dead center and slashed it sideways, wrenching away the bio-cables to yank out his own heart.

As he thrust the stone in Harvey's direction like one final gesture of spite, his figure grew steadily farther and farther away—

Harvey heard a crash somewhere far down below.

He could see the sky.

Far, far beyond the peaked-hat roofs of the steeples, the sky growing tinged with the copper of evening ran from one end of the world to the other high, high above. The planet's sky, blurred with fine clouds of dust. A sky so much lower than it seemed, and yet he knew that his hands could never reach it.

Blah…am I still alive, then?

His right hand, lying flung out against the ground, still held his own heart.

What did you want?

There hadn't been anything he'd wanted anywhere, really. In the end he'd only been grasping after something that didn't exist and that he didn't even understand, so it was only natural that he'd never been able to get it, no matter how far he went or how high he climbed.

Yeah, but just now, he'd figured a little of it out……*I wanted to be like him. He's a freakishly softhearted moron, he can't make up his mind about anything, he's totally hopeless—but that's probably why he somehow wound up with all kinds of things I couldn't get no matter how much I wanted them.*

Yeah, yeah, that's right. I was jealous of you all along…

Our starting lines would have been the same—what made our paths split off in different directions? Where did I step wrong?

If I didn't step off the path, I—

It seemed like kind of a shame that this was how it ended, just when he thought he was finally starting to get an idea of what he'd wanted. *It's been one long, pointless life, huh. Oh, well. A pointless, dumbass death like this suits me.*

He raised his right hand and grabbed at the sky.

Not even the tips of his fingers could reach it, naturally, and then—

Plop. His heart slipped out of his palm and rolled away along the rocky ground.

His copper-stained field of vision turned steadily white. There was nothing there; no light or sound or smell, no loneliness or despair or suffering or sorrow or even pleasure.

There was really nothing at all there at the end of the world.

It was a really, really immaculate nothingness.

IN PLACE OF AN AFTERWORD

Hello. I'm Yuka-ako Kabei (what kind of character is this?).

......Okay, the thing is, because of how the volume ended, I really struggled with how to connect the afterword to it, and so I ended up with this weird hyperactive vibe that just destroys any lingering aftertones of the story that you may be savoring...I-I'm sorry.

Right, so I've managed to present you with the eighth volume of *Kieli*. This volume is a little bit different from the previous volumes. What's different, you ask? There are different characters on the cover. Taue-san put a lot of spirit into it. And what with one thing and another, somewhere along the way this volume ended up featuring Joachim as the shadow protagonist.

And now the next volume will be the final one. The *Kieli* series is set to total out at nine volumes, just like my wishful thinking in the last volume's afterword.

Um, I think it would be tasteless to talk at length about the content of the story at this point...so let's consider this particular afterword a "special episode." I'd like to take this time to answer the most frequently asked questions in the letters my fine readers have sent me. Look, my pretty much running out of stuff to talk about in the afterwords is, uh...not what's happening here, okay?

And now, let the Q&A fest begin.

Q. Can't I listen to the radio drama you wrote about in Volume VI's afterword anymore?

A. Unfortunately, the radio drama broadcast is over, but it's been released as a drama CD, with everything from the broadcast plus a bonus track. It also comes with a bonus short story, and it's chock-full of original illustrations by Taue-san, so I'd love for you to give it a listen. As of now (February 2006), I think it's in stock at Animates nationwide and at Dengeki's online shop (www.dengekiya.com).

Q. Did you really handwrite the message on the postcard reply to my fan letter, Ms. Kabei?

A. Absolutely! Incidentally, when I asked someone living with me, "Don't you think my handwriting is a little too messy to show other people?" they answered, "Your writing is beyond the dimension of 'good handwriting' or 'bad handwriting' and into chicken-scratch territory." I'm sorry my messages are always chicken-scratching... Also, I always write my draft manuscripts on five-millimeter graph paper and cram in the words really tight, so my lettering is super-tiny...

Q. Where does the accent go in Harvey's name?

A. I was surprised by how many people asked this question (you see, I never had any doubts about pronouncing it...). I think you can tell how it goes if you listen to the drama CD, but, um, it's difficult to explain on paper... It's the same accent pattern as when you shout "mambo [sunfish]!" (What kind of example is that?) Or "senbei [rice cracker]" or "mocho [appendix]," or "Kancho [Captain]!" in response to "I'll go down with the ship" or something.

*   *   *

Q. Please tell us the Corporal's real name.
A. That's a secret.

....

Listen, it's not that I never *decided* on a name, okay?

....

Q. Please tell us your dog's name.
A. It's "Yukichi." You see, I like the sound "yu." A lot of my characters have "ya" or "yu" or "yo" in their names, too.

Q. Reading Volume V and Volume VI, I started to like Joachim.
A. Thank you. *grins broadly* As the writer, he was a favorite of mine, too, because I found it very easy to write his subtle insanity.

Q. I'd like to be a novelist someday. Do you have any advice?
A. Urk…I go through a trial-and-error process writing each book, so I can't give anything worth calling "advice"… Well, I think one way of training yourself is to just write the whole thing to the end and not chuck it partway through. Because you realize very different things from getting sick of it and quitting with it half-done versus using every ounce of tenacity you've got to power through to that last scene. Other than that, I think having plenty of fun with your friends and absorbing lots of things outside the realm of novels is the most

valuable thing... though now that I've graduated, I regret having spent my school days goofing off... I hope I'll have the pleasure of meeting you as a colleague one day. Give it your best! (I-I'd better give it my best, too, so that I can keep my career as a novelist until then.)

Q. Won't *Kieli* be made into a manga or anime?

A. It recently got a manga adaptation! It's been running in Akita Shoten's manga magazine *Mystery Bonita* (which comes out on the 6th of each month) since December 2005. The manga artist, Shiori Teshirogi, draws wonderful art that's a bit different in style from Taue-san's (plus she's got a fetish for old abandoned buildings, just like me, so we're kindred spirits!). I highly encourage you check out this other *Kieli* world.

Q. Please keep writing *Kieli* forever!

A. Many people have been kind enough to say things like that. Thank you all very much. But you see, I think stories really ought to have endings... If you follow this story all this way to its final volume, that will be the greatest happiness I could ask for.

All right, I hope to be able to see you again in *The Dead Sleep Eternally in the Wilderness, Part 2.*

Yukako Kabei